TRAPPED BY
VIALLI'S VOWS

TRAPPED BY VIALLI'S VOWS

BY

CHANTELLE SHAW

HarperCollins
PUBLISHERS
Since 1817

First published in Great Britain 2016
By Mills & Boon, an imprint of HarperCollins*Publishers*
1 London Bridge Street, London, SE1 9GF

Large Print edition 2017

© 2016 Chantelle Shaw

ISBN: 978-0-263-07046-0

Printed and bound in Great Britain
by CPI Antony Rowe, Chippenham, Wiltshire

CHAPTER ONE

'SO YOU'RE LEANDRO'S dirty little secret.'

Marnie jerked her gaze from the door of the restaurant—she'd been watching it for Leandro's arrival—to the man who had sat down on the bar stool next to her. She wondered if she had misheard him.

'I'm sorry?'

He grinned and held out his hand. 'Forgive my little joke. I'm Fergus Leary, senior accountant at Vialli Entertainment. Everyone in the company is curious about why Leandro keeps his girlfriend hidden. We only heard of your existence when he asked his PA to phone you about the party.'

Marnie tried to ignore the sinking feeling in the pit of her stomach. She had taken an immediate dislike to Fergus, but smiled politely. At least the accountant had spoken to her, which was more than any of Leandro's other staff had done. She had felt nervous enough when she'd arrived alone at the restaurant which had been booked for the private party, and the curious glances she'd received from the other guests had made her feel worse.

Like her, everyone seemed to be waiting for Leandro. He was fifteen minutes late and, although she'd tried calling him, his phone was constantly busy. There was nothing new in that, Marnie thought ruefully. She had only spoken to him a few times in the past two weeks while he had been away on a business trip to New York.

'Leandro gets frustrated with the paparazzi's constant attention so we avoid popular restaurants and bars,' she explained to Fergus.

In fact lately she *had* wondered why Leandro never asked her to accompany him to social events, such as the star-studded film premiere he'd attended the previous week.

'I'm going to the premiere because it's a good business opportunity and a chance to network,' he'd told her when, for the first time in their relationship, Marnie had queried why he hadn't invited her to go with him.

'You won't know anyone, and I'm sure you would be bored.' Her disappointment must have shown on her face, because then he had said in a conciliatory tone, 'We'll go out for dinner when I get back from New York. In fact we'll have a weekend away somewhere. Choose where you want to go and I'll make the arrangements. How about Prague? You've often said you would like to visit the city.'

He had avoided further discussion by taking her to bed, but later, after he had fallen asleep, Marnie had realised that yet again he had distracted her with the promise of a trip away together and sex—which always reassured her that although their relationship might be unconventional she was extremely happy living with Leandro and he seemed equally content.

The fact that she was here at this party he was giving for his staff from Vialli Entertainment, to celebrate the completed refurbishments of his latest theatre project, was proof that he had listened to her small complaint about their relationship and invited her. Admittedly he must have made a last-minute decision to include her, and he had left it to his PA to relay to Marnie the details of the venue and the time of the party.

Determined to dress to impress for her first public appearance with Leandro, she had shopped for a new outfit on Bond Street. But it had been an unenjoyable experience—not only because the price labels on the clothes had seriously stretched her overdraft, but memories of the humiliating incident when she was eighteen and had been accused of shoplifting from a big department store had made her feel tense while she'd been trying on outfits.

If she had spent a bit longer looking in the mirror at the boutique, rather than being in a rush to change back into her own clothes, she might have noticed that the dress was a fraction too tight, she thought as she caught sight of her reflection in the mirror behind the bar. The black velvet dress clung to her hourglass figure, which was more curvaceous since she had gained a few pounds recently. She hoped that the string of pearls around her throat would detract attention from the dress's plunging neckline.

Glancing around the restaurant, she noted that all the female members of Leandro's staff were slimmer and more sophisticated than her. Self-doubt gripped her. When she had first met Leandro, at the cocktail bar and restaurant where she worked, one of the other waitresses had told her that he had a reputation as a playboy who liked to date beautiful models and socialites. Marnie knew, realistically, that she was only averagely attractive, and she had never understood why Leandro had chosen her for his lover when he could have had any woman he wanted.

A flurry of activity on the other side of the restaurant caught her attention, and her heart leapt when the door opened and Leandro Vialli strode in.

Nothing about his lean, lithe, jaw-droppingly handsome appearance indicated that he had stepped off a long-haul flight less than an hour ago. He would have flown from New York on his private jet, before travelling to the restaurant in his chauffeur-driven Bentley, and he looked like a model from a glossy magazine.

The cut of his jacket revealed the width of his broad shoulders and his tapered trousers moulded his muscular thighs and emphasised his long legs. His golden tanned complexion and the thick mahogany hair swept back from his brow indicated his Mediterranean heritage, although he spoke with a faint American drawl.

The tabloids called him an Italian playboy, while the broadsheets reported on his meteoric career success. Leandro owned several West End theatres and was responsible for restoring some of the most historically important venues in London. And Vialli Entertainment was only an offshoot of his property development giant Vialli Holdings in New York—one of the top businesses in the US with a portfolio worth billions.

His hard-boned features revealed nothing of his thoughts, but the cynical curve of his lips spoke of a man who was confident in his abilities and dismissive of fools. He exuded an air of power and charisma that sent a thrill of excitement through Marnie.

She had missed him desperately while he had been away, and she wanted to run towards him and throw herself into his arms. But she restrained the impulse, aware that Leandro disliked public displays of emotion. The thought came into her mind that even when they were alone he kept his emotions under tight control, and only when they made love did his reserved air sometimes crack.

She slid off the bar stool and ran a hand through her long blonde hair. Her mouth curved into a smile—which faltered as Leandro's steel-grey gaze raked the room and an expression of surprise followed by one of irritation flickered on his face when he saw her. In that moment the uncertainty that had plagued Marnie lately settled like wet concrete in the pit of her stomach.

Five days ago it had been the first anniversary of when they had become lovers, but Leandro hadn't phoned from New York to wish her happy anniversary. When he had called a day later she had felt reluctant to remind him of the significant date, although she'd harboured a secret hope that he was planning to celebrate their anniversary when he came home. But Leandro did not look in a celebratory mood as he strode towards her.

He was probably tired after his journey. She ignored the thought that he had amazing energy and an insatiable libido and could make love to her several times a night. She would *not* let her insecurities—which she suspected stemmed from having been abandoned by her father when she was a child—spoil what she had with Leandro, Marnie told herself firmly.

Her heart skipped a beat when he halted in front of her. The familiar spicy scent of his aftershave teased her senses and her insides melted. Despite the fact that she was wearing four-inch heels she had to tilt her head to meet his distinctly cool gaze.

'*Cara*, I wasn't expecting to see you here.'

'But you invited me…didn't you?' Her voice faltered as her heart plummeted. 'Your PA phoned me yesterday and said you had asked her to let me know about the party.'

Leandro frowned. 'My *actual* instruction to Julie was to inform you that the date of the staff party had been brought forward from next week to this evening because the restaurant had made a mistake with the booking. I was involved in important negotiations in New York and couldn't phone you myself, but I wanted to warn you that I wouldn't be home until late tonight.'

'I see.'

Humiliation swept in a tide of heated colour across Marnie's face. With a few devastating words Leandro had forced her to acknowledge the holes in their relationship. She had made excuses—he was a busy executive and so couldn't spend as much time with her as she would have liked. She had told herself it didn't matter that he had forgotten their anniversary. But with a flash of clarity she saw that she had been fooling herself.

She wished the ground would open up and swallow her. But as she searched his hard-boned face for some small sign of softness anger surged through her, as heated as it was unexpected. Usually she avoided confrontation, but she was overwhelmed by a storm of wild emotions. Surely it wasn't unreasonable to want to be included in

Leandro's social life, considering they had been in a relationship for a year?

'Obviously if I'd realised that you hadn't invited me to the party I wouldn't have come,' she said in a low voice, aware that they were the focus of attention of many of Leandro's staff.

But for once her temper refused to be suppressed as she remembered Fergus's comment. *Leandro's dirty little secret*. Was that how everyone at the party thought of her? Was it how Leandro thought of her?

'Are you ashamed of me?' she burst out.

'Don't be ridiculous.' His clipped tone revealed his displeasure.

'What else am I supposed to think when you never want to be seen in public with me?' Her voice rose and Leandro's warning frown intensified her anger. At the same time she was secretly shocked that she was arguing with him, or at least trying to goad him, but he refused to respond, although his lips thinned into a stern line.

Memories of her mother screaming wild accusations at her father sent a shudder through her.

Oh, God, was she turning into a hysterical, irrational woman like her mother had been? She wasn't imagining that people were looking at her. Leandro's hard-boned features gave no clue to his thoughts, but Marnie sensed from the taut way he held his body that he was surprised by her behaviour, and the steely gleam in his grey eyes told her he was furious.

Her excitement about attending the party with him congealed into a hard knot of misery in her chest. With a choked cry she stepped past him—and stiffened when he placed his hand on her arm.

'Where are you going?'

'I'm not staying at the party now I know that you don't want me to be here.' She couldn't disguise the wobble in her voice. 'What does it matter where I'm going? It's not as if you care.'

The truth of that last statement felt like a punch in her gut. She shook her arm free from his grasp and walked as quickly as her high heels would allow across the restaurant. She half expected him to follow her, and her heart sank when he didn't.

* * *

Leandro watched Marnie's curvaceous figure march away from him and felt a tightening sensation in his groin as he admired the sexy sway of her derriere. He could not actually believe she would walk out on him, and he was puzzled as much as irritated when she exited the restaurant.

She was not prone to temper tantrums—unlike his ex-wife. Marnie was easy-going, and could always be relied upon to agree with him. He appreciated a life without the drama that had been a feature of his marriage, but he had to admit that he was intrigued to discover an unexpected fiery side to her character. Recalling her hurt expression, he cursed his tactlessness. But he did not like surprises, and he'd been shocked when he'd walked into the restaurant and spotted her.

He would have to have words with Julie, who was covering for his usual PA, Fiona, while she was on maternity leave. But he knew he couldn't blame the temp for the misunderstanding over inviting Marnie to the staff party. He should have made sure that Julie understood that he never mixed his public and private life—and his mistress belonged firmly in the latter category.

He had made it clear to Marnie when they had met that all he wanted was a no-strings affair. His suspicion that she was a virgin had been allayed by her white-hot passion when they'd slept together for the first time. It had blown his mind. But sex was all he wanted from her and the only thing he could offer.

He had tried commitment once, and had his soul ripped out for his efforts, Leandro thought grimly. His marriage had quickly become a farce that had ultimately turned ugly, and he had no intention of repeating the biggest mistake of his life, despite his father's nagging.

He'd had dinner with Silvestro Vialli while he'd been in New York and the old man had gone on about him marrying again and, more importantly as far as his father was concerned, producing an heir to secure the future of Vialli Holdings. Leandro had learned early in life that business was the only thing his father cared about.

'Next time make sure you have a paternity

test to prove the child is yours as soon as it's born, so you avoid the disaster that happened last time,' Silvestro had advised with typical bluntness.

But there wasn't going to be a next time. Nicole's deception had left deep scars, and nothing would persuade Leandro to be metaphorically manacled to a woman for the rest of his life. Memories of his parents' volatile marriage and bitter divorce when he was seven reinforced his belief that commitment was a mug's game. He wasn't interested in a long-term relationship— which made the fact that Marnie had been his mistress for a year all the more shocking.

He couldn't comprehend how their affair had lasted for so long without him noticing that she had stealthily infiltrated his life. It was certainly not what he'd intended when he had made a spur-of-the-moment decision to ask her to move in with him nearly a year ago. She had needed somewhere to live, and he had assumed he would grow bored with her in a matter of weeks and would find her another flat to move into.

He was unsettled by the realisation that he had

not been tempted by another woman since he'd made Marnie his mistress.

A waiter offered him champagne and canapés. Leandro lifted a glass from the tray and took a long sip, needing the hit of alcohol in his blood-stream. His schedule in New York had been hell-ish, even by his standards, but he always pushed himself to his limits. He was proud of Vialli Entertainment, the business he had built with-out the support or help of his father. Work was central to his existence and gave him a sense of control that in the past few years had been miss-ing from other areas of his life.

After his marriage had failed he had focused on being a good father, determined that Henry would not suffer from the divorce the way he had done when he was a kid and his own par-ents had split up. But since he'd received the devastating proof that Henry wasn't his son he had been left with a void inside him where his heart had once been, and he had vowed never to lay himself open to that level of pain ever again.

His father had spent his life avoiding making emotional attachments, Leandro thought cynically. It was the only trait of Silvestro's that he was determined to emulate. His mother, on the other hand, had fallen in love dozens of times, with men who had broken her heart, but she hadn't loved the one person who had adored her—her son.

Leandro forced his thoughts back to the present and Marnie's unexpected behaviour. What the hell had got into her? He hadn't tried to stop her from leaving the party because he'd been concerned that she would create a scene in front of his staff. But that was shocking in itself, because generally she was mild natured and until recently had seemed content to take a backstage role in his life.

He frowned as he recalled that when he had phoned her from New York a couple of days ago she had sounded odd, unlike her usual cheerful self. He had almost been tempted to ask if something had upset her. But he hadn't gone down that route, reminding himself that she was his mistress and he neither sought nor offered to share personal confidences with her.

It might be a good thing that she had demonstrated this volatile side to her character, he brooded. He was frankly stunned that he had allowed their affair to continue for a year, and if Marnie was going to start making emotional demands on him it was time to think about replacing her in his bed.

He was aware that several of his senior staff were trying to catch his attention and told himself to forget about Marnie and enjoy the party. But he had glimpsed the sparkle of tears in her eyes before she'd hurried away from him and his conscience was pricked.

He guessed she would take a cab back to his house in Chelsea because she had nowhere else to go. She had told him that her mother had died a few months before they'd met and her only other relatives lived in Norfolk.

Leandro gulped down the rest of his champagne and swore beneath his breath. Experience had taught him that women were nothing but trouble, and he did not know why he was surprised that Marnie was no different from all the rest. She wasn't his responsibility, but she was upset, and he acknowledged that he was partly to blame.

He walked over to his deputy CEO and spoke to him briefly before he phoned his chauffeur and requested to be collected from the party.

Marnie emerged from the air-conditioned restaurant into what felt like a furnace. The summer heatwave had lasted for weeks, and London was sweltering in unusually high temperatures. Even at eight o'clock in the evening the sun was a burning golden disc in the sky, and she was conscious of her dress sticking to her as she walked dispiritedly towards the bus stop.

She couldn't believe she had stormed out of the party like that. Leandro had looked shocked by her loss of temper and it was hardly surprising that he had not followed her after she had yelled at him like a fishwife.

More tears filled her eyes. What was *wrong* with her? She never cried.

Even when her brother Luke had been killed in a motorbike accident she had bottled up her grief, and maybe that was why she still felt his loss acutely, five years later. Growing up with her chronically depressed mother had made her fearful of allowing herself to feel deep emotions. She was scared that if she cried for Luke she might never be able to stop. Besides, she'd had to stay strong for her other brother, Jake, who had been devastated by his twin's death. And she had done her best to take care of her mother, as she had done since she was eleven, when her father had left home.

She leaned against the bus shelter and gave a deep sigh. This past year that she had lived with Leandro had been the happiest time she'd known since she was a child, when her family had still been together. But even back then there had been problems in her parents' marriage. Memories of her parents' frequent rows, when her dad had accused her mum of smothering him with her possessiveness, had taught Marnie that she must give Leandro space.

She had certainly tried to do that. It occurred to her that she knew barely any more about him now than when they had first met. He had never introduced her to his friends or family, and the only pieces of personal information he had revealed were that his father lived in New York and his mother had been a famous musical theatre star who had died ten years ago.

She did not know why it suddenly mattered that Leandro kept so much of his private life secret from her. She'd been prone to odd mood swings lately, and maybe that explained why she felt so hurt by his cavalier treatment of her. But her forgiving nature was quick to point out that he was a millionaire business tycoon who had a high-octane lifestyle and he couldn't make her his top priority all the time.

She had been looking forward to his return from New York because she was excited about telling him her amazing news. It was still hard to believe that not only had she gained a first-class honours degree in astrophysics, but had earned the highest exam marks in the country. Leandro would certainly be surprised. She chewed on her lip. Maybe she should have told him before now that for the past year she had worked only one day a week as a waitress in the cocktail bar, and on the other days had studied astronomy, space science and astrophysics at a top London university.

Marnie heard her mother's voice in her mind. *'Why do you want to study astronomy? What's the use in looking at stars and planets? You need to train for a proper job instead of setting your sights on an impossible dream.'*

The teachers at the rough comprehensive school she'd attended had been similarly dismissive of her chances of becoming an astronomer, but she had worked hard at school and ignored the bullies who had called her a geek because she'd enjoyed science lessons. Even though she had been accepted at a top university back then she had lacked confidence in her abilities, and she'd decided to wait to see if she passed her final exams before she told Leandro about her dream of becoming an astronomer.

Now that dream was a step closer to being fulfilled. She had been offered a place on an internship programme to study towards a doctoral degree at NASA's research academy in California. It would necessitate her moving to the States temporarily, and she hoped Leandro would understand that they would have to have a long-distance relationship for nine months while she was studying in America.

Marnie glanced along the road, hoping to see a bus approaching. Her heart lurched when a black saloon car with dark-tinted windows drew up against the pavement and the rear door opened. Leandro's face was shadowed in the dim interior of the car, but his steel-grey eyes gleamed with hard brilliance.

'Get in the car, Marnie.'

She almost sagged with relief that he had come after her. But the rebellious streak that seemed to be intent on causing trouble argued that she could not allow him to continue to walk all over her, that she should stand up for herself a bit more because she did not want to be his 'dirty little secret'.

While she hesitated, Leandro drawled, 'I will only ask you once, *cara*.'

CHAPTER TWO

MARNIE DID NOT look at Leandro as she slid onto the back seat of the car beside him and shut the door. He instructed the chauffeur to drive on before he closed the privacy glass. The tension between them was almost tangible, and she knotted her fingers together in her lap, determined that she was not going to be the first to speak.

'What the hell was *that* about?' He did not try to hide his irritation. 'I didn't invite you to the staff party because I had planned to show my face for an hour at most before I rushed home to you.'

It was partially true, and Leandro realised he had to smooth over an awkward situation. His eyes were drawn to the jerky rise and fall of Marnie's breasts, which appeared to be in imminent danger of escaping from the plunging neckline of her dress. Her skin was peaches and cream and her honey-blonde hair rippled half-way down her back. A shaft of unadulterated lust swept through him as he imagined undressing her and cupping her ripe curves in his hands.

'Really?'

She sounded uncertain, and Leandro stifled his impatience to push her back against the leather seat and cover her mouth with his.

'We could have spent time together at the party,' Marnie muttered. She had felt really hurt by Leandro's attitude and for once was determined not to allow him to brush her feelings aside as if they didn't matter.

'I spend a significant chunk of my life in the company of the people I work with and I won't apologise for wanting to spend my leisure time exclusively with you.'

'Oh.' When he put it like that his decision not to invite her to the party sounded reasonable. Perhaps she *had* overreacted a bit.

Leandro closed his hand over hers, and as Marnie looked down at his tanned fingers wrapped around her paler ones she pictured his naked limbs entwined with hers, dark against pale, hard against soft.

She was intensely aware of his hard thigh muscles pressed up against her. He reached out and wrapped a lock of her long hair around his finger, and her breath became trapped in her throat when he gently tugged to make her turn her head towards him. The hard gleam in his eyes had been replaced with a sultry smokiness that turned her bones to liquid.

Leandro felt Marnie relax and was confident he had won her over. His hunger became more urgent as he tipped her chin up and plundered her soft, moist lips without mercy, wanting to punish her just a little and remind her that *he* called the shots in their affair.

Her eager response fanned the flames of his desire. He had taught her well, and she was no longer shy and inexperienced as she had been in the early days of their affair. When she pushed her tongue into his mouth his heart slammed against his ribs, his desire a potent force that strained against the zip of his trousers.

Lifting his head, Leandro was satisfied to see

rosy colour on her cheeks, and saw that her blush continued down her throat and spread a warm stain over the upper slopes of her breasts. This was how he had pictured his mistress while he was away: flushed with desire and her brown eyes soft with sensual promise.

Leandro's words had allayed some of Marnie's concerns that their relationship did not mean as much to him as it did to her. She rested her hand on the bulge beneath his trousers and smiled when he groaned. 'Did you miss me while you were away?'

'Of course I missed you.' He gave a rough laugh. 'After two weeks without sex I am seriously frustrated, *cara.*'

'I wasn't only talking about sex.'

But her tiny flicker of doubt wavered as he crushed her to him and sought her mouth again, kissing her with a possessive intent that thrilled her. Passion ignited into an inferno between them and she forgot everything but the need to feel his hands on her body.

He pushed her back against the leather seat

and leaned over her. '*Dio*, I've wanted this so badly,' he said thickly.

Marnie allowed herself to sink into the bliss of Leandro's kiss. Too many nights without him had made her body extra-responsive, and she gave a low moan when he slipped his hand into the front of her dress and stroked her breasts through her sheer lace bra. When he rolled her nipples between his fingers she almost leapt off the seat as starbursts of pleasure arrowed down from her breasts to the hot, moist core of her femininity.

He gave a husky laugh. '*This* is what I missed. Your beautiful body, ready and eager for me. I'm impatient to get you home so that I can undress you.' He traced the neckline of her dress with his forefinger. 'Is this a new dress? Did you buy it for the party? When I walked into the restaurant I was blown away by how sexy you looked.'

She remembered how unsure of herself she had felt while she had waited for Leandro to arrive at the restaurant. If he felt proud of her, perhaps she would feel more his equal.

'Leandro,' she murmured, when he tore his

mouth from hers to allow them to draw breath. 'Do you wish I had a better job than waitressing?'

'There's nothing wrong with being a waitress,' he said indistinctly, busy nibbling her earlobe before trailing his lips down her throat and moving purposefully towards her cleavage.

'But wouldn't you like me to have a high-flying career, like the women you employ at your company?' she persisted.

'I've dated career women, and to be frank it was a nightmare trying to align our schedules and arrange to meet when we happened to be on the same continent. I like knowing that you're at home waiting for me when I get back from work.'

Marnie was disappointed by Leandro's apparent lack of enthusiasm for her to have a career, but at the same time her foolish heart quivered because he'd said that he looked forward to coming home to her every evening. She drew an unsteady breath when he eased the stretchy neckline of her dress and her bra down and cupped her breasts in his palms, so that he could flick his tongue across one nipple and then the other.

The sensation of him sucking each tender peak was electrifying.

Dazed with desire, she decided to wait and tell him about the opportunity she had been offered to study astronomy at NASA until later—after they had assuaged their hunger for each other that was now at fever pitch after their two-week separation.

Leandro pulled her onto his lap and thrust his hand beneath her skirt to stroke the strip of sensitive bare skin above the lace band of her stocking tops. Shivering with longing, she let her thighs fall open to allow him to move his hand higher, to the place where she longed for him to touch her.

'You *are* hungry,' he drawled, satisfaction thickening his voice as he eased his finger beneath her thong and discovered the slick wetness of her arousal.

A voice in the back of Marnie's mind taunted her, telling her that her weakness for Leandro was shameful. She didn't want to appear needy, but the truth was she *did* need him. Before she had met him she'd felt empty and alone.

He pushed another finger into her and moved his hand with rhythmical strokes, in and out, faster, deeper, taking her higher until she couldn't think of anything but the beauty of what he was doing to her.

'Leandro…' She clung to his shoulders as she felt the first exquisite spasms of her orgasm.

'That's right, baby. Come for me,' he said thickly.

Overwhelmed with pleasure, she pressed her face into his neck and breathed in the spicy scent of his aftershave. Her heart clenched with emotion. She had missed him so much, and from the size of the rock-hard erection she could feel beneath her bottom he had missed her as badly.

Minutes later the car drew up in Eaton Square and Marnie quickly tugged her dress into place before the chauffeur opened the door. Leandro kept his arm around her waist, as if he knew that her legs felt unsteady, and they hurried up the steps of the house.

As they entered the hallway he kicked the front door shut and pulled her against his hard body, his hands roaming over her with feverish urgency. He curled his fingers into the soft mounds of her buttocks before running a hand up her spine and unzipping her dress. With his help the black velvet slipped down to expose her semi-sheer bra, through which her dusky nipples were clearly visible.

Leandro gave a growl that sent a shiver of anticipation through Marnie. She wanted him *now*—this minute.

He must have sensed her desperation, because he lifted her and sat her on the marble table in the hall, pushed her skirt up to her thighs.

'I can't wait long enough for us to get upstairs to the bedroom,' he said hoarsely.

Her heart lurched when she saw the feral hunger in his eyes. But a familiar sound that she had grown to hate shattered the sizzling sexual tension.

'Your damned phone!' she muttered.

'I'll switch it off,' he promised.

But as he pulled his mobile phone out of his jacket pocket he glanced at the screen and stiffened.

'*Cara*, I'm sorry, but I have to take this.'

'You can't be serious…' She almost wept with frustration, but her sense of hurt and abandonment was even worse than the unfulfilled ache between her legs as she watched him stride into his study and close the door behind him, shutting her out of his life—as usual, Marnie thought bitterly.

But he was the head of a multi-million-pound company and sometimes he *had* to deal with business matters at unsociable hours, she reminded herself. She recognised that he was speaking French—which was another surprise, because she hadn't known that he was fluent in the language. There were so many things she did not know about Leandro.

She slid down from the table and readjusted her dress. Her breasts ached and she felt a little bit sick. She recalled that she'd felt nauseous at about the same time on the previous few evenings and wondered if it had something to do with the heatwave. Maybe she needed to drink more water.

Leandro's voice was still audible through the study door. Marnie wandered into the sitting room. Like all the rooms in the house, its modern décor was a contrast to the building's imposing Georgian façade. The walls and furnishings were in neutral tones and a few pieces of contemporary and no doubt very expensive artwork added splashes of bold colour.

It was a curiously impersonal room, but Leandro had told her that he had employed interior designers to decorate the house, which perhaps explained why there was no stamp of his personality anywhere. When she had moved in with him Marnie had placed a couple of potted ferns on the windowsill to try and breathe some life into the room, but they looked as out of place as she felt.

She stood by the window and watched the shadows lengthen in the private gardens at the centre of the square. The district of Belgravia was very different from the council estate where she'd grown up. She had moved there, to one of the most deprived parts of south London, with her mother and brothers after her dad had left and their family home had been sold. The Silden Estate had been notorious for gang crime and drug dealing, and one reason why she had wanted a good career was so that she could escape the sense of hopelessness that had pervaded the estate.

Marnie remembered that when she'd first met Leandro she had told herself he was out of her league. He had been a regular customer at the cocktail bar and restaurant where she worked and she hadn't taken his flirting seriously—until one night when he had asked her out to dinner.

It had been the first time she'd been on a proper dinner date, and to start with she had felt on edge, but he had soon put her at her ease with his charismatic charm. By the end of the evening she had fallen completely under his spell and had needed little persuading to spend the night with him.

She did not know if he had guessed that he was her first lover. Up until then she hadn't had time for boyfriends. She'd been too busy studying, working and looking after her mother, whose depression had worsened after Luke had died and Jake had disappeared. But following her mother's death she had felt a sense of freedom from responsibility, and when Leandro had asked her to move in with him she'd fallen head-long into their passionate affair.

Marnie sighed. In those early days it hadn't worried her that Leandro worked long hours, or that the only time they spent together was in bed. She'd enjoyed having sex with him—she still did. But although the situation was the same she realised that *she* had changed. She had fallen in love with him, and she was seeking clues that would indicate how he felt about her.

Up until he had gone to New York she had be-lieved that he felt something more for her than sexual attraction. But his attitude towards her at the party and the ease with which he had dis-missed her and answered the phone had reawak-ened her doubts about their relationship.

The study door was open when Marnie walked past again, and she saw that the room was empty. She hurried up the stairs and her heart gave a little skip as she headed into the master bedroom that she shared with Leandro. Now that he had finished his phone call there would hopefully be no more interruptions to prevent him making love to her.

They communicated best in bed. Their passion for each other made words unnecessary when their bodies were in perfect accord. But for her it wasn't just about sex. She craved the feeling of closeness when he held her in his arms and stroked her hair. When he was tender she could convince herself that he cared about her.

As she entered the bedroom Leandro walked out of the en suite bathroom, naked apart from the towel hitched around his hips. Droplets of water clung to the whorls of dark hair that covered his chest. It was his habit to shower before they had sex, and Marnie's mouth went dry as her eyes followed the path of his body hair as it arrowed over his flat stomach and she visualised his powerful manhood beneath the towel.

But while she stared, and tried to control her thundering pulse, he opened a drawer, took out a pair of silk boxer shorts and returned to the bathroom, emerging moments later wearing the boxers.

Marnie's disappointment turned to confusion

as she watched him pull on a pair of jeans. She froze when she noticed a suitcase on the bed. 'Are you…going somewhere?'

He finished buttoning his shirt and spared her a brief glance. 'Paris.'

'Now? Tonight?' She couldn't accept what her eyes were telling her as she watched him throw a few other items of clothing into the case. *'Why?'* Her insecurity about their relationship made her voice sharp. 'You went to Paris the weekend before you flew to New York.'

In fact he visited Paris regularly, once a month, and spent the weekend there. She assumed he went for business reasons, but he had never given any explanation for his trips and she had not dared ask him, telling herself that she mustn't crowd him or seem possessive.

Another thought struck her. 'Have you remembered that we're going to Norfolk for my cousin's wedding?'

'I'm afraid I won't be able to go with you.'

She couldn't disguise her disappointment. 'But you *said* you would come—and I've told Gemma that I'm bringing an additional guest.'

'I said I would *try* to keep the date of the wedding free but I didn't promise,' Leandro said tersely. He raked a hand through his hair. 'I'm going to Paris because a…a close friend has been injured in an accident and I need to be with them.'

Marnie looked at him and noticed the lines of strain around his mouth. It was so unlike him to show any emotion, and she immediately felt guilty that she had doubted him. 'I'm sorry. Is your friend seriously hurt?'

She refused to listen to the voice in her head that questioned whether Leandro considered *her* to be a close friend. Would he drop everything if she was hurt and rush to be with *her*?

'I don't have many details.' He sounded distracted. 'I just had the phone call…' He gave her a wry glance as he referred to their interrupted lovemaking downstairs. 'I'm sorry I have to rush off, and I'm sorry about your cousin's wedding. I can't say yet when I'll be home.'

This from a man who organised his life with military precision. It made Marnie realise how worried Leandro must be. 'It doesn't matter. Of course you must go to your friend. Is there anything I can do to help?' she asked softly.

He closed the zip on his suitcase and reached for his jacket. 'Can you grab my phone? I must have left it in the bathroom.'

His mobile bleeped as she picked it up from the vanity unit and she could not help but notice the words on the screen.

You have a message from Stephanie.

Who was Stephanie? A member of his staff? Another friend?

For a split second Marnie was tempted to read his messages. Then a memory from her childhood, when she had seen her mother searching the pockets of her father's jacket for proof that he was seeing another woman, made her feel sickened with herself. Leandro had never given her a reason not to trust him. She could not bear the idea that she might have inherited her mother's suspicious nature, and she hurried back into the bedroom and thrust his phone at him as if it had burned her hand.

She followed him over to the door and her soft

heart ached with sympathy when he pushed his hair back from his brow in a weary gesture.

'You must be tired after travelling from a different time zone. I hope your friend is okay.'

'Thanks.' He bent his head and brushed his mouth across hers.

She responded instantly, her lips softening and clinging just a little when he tried to break the kiss. He hesitated, and looked at her with an odd expression on his face. Marnie sensed he was about to say something, but then the moment passed and the connection she had felt with him shattered as he turned and strode down the hall.

Leandro's driver opened the car door for him before stowing his suitcase in the boot. 'The pilot has the plane ready, sir. It's a busy night for you—off abroad again only a few hours after you arrived back in England.'

'You're telling me,' Leandro muttered.

As the car pulled away from the kerb he leaned his head against the back of the seat and took a deep breath. God, he hoped Henry was all right. A suspected broken collarbone, the headmaster of Henry's school in Paris had said on the phone. Apparently the boy had been on an adventure hiking trip with some classmates and had slipped and fallen down a steep gully. Due to the remote location, it had taken a few hours to transport Henry to a hospital in Paris.

Henry's injury wasn't life-threatening, but Leandro knew it must be incredibly painful. He remembered that he had dislocated his collarbone playing rugby when he was about twelve and it had been agony. His father had been away on a business trip and his mother had been performing somewhere else in the world, so he had been left on his own at the hospital to receive treatment for his injury before one of his father's staff had collected him and taken him back to the penthouse apartment on Fifth Avenue that had never felt like a home to Leandro.

He hated the thought of Henry being in pain and maybe feeling scared and alone. Nicole was abroad, which was why the school had phoned Leandro—he was listed as an emergency contact for Henry. He suspected that his ex-wife only allowed him to maintain a relationship with Henry because it suited her, he thought cynically.

Leandro's thoughts turned to Marnie. He could not explain why he had felt an urge to tell her that the friend he was rushing to visit in Paris was a ten-year-old boy whom his ex-wife had led him to believe was his son for six years. But the desire to confide in Marnie had only lasted for a few moments, before his brain had taken charge and reminded him that he had never shared personal information with any of his previous mistresses, so why would he with her?

He deliberately did not bring his emotions into his affairs. Just because his affair with Marnie had lasted longer than his affairs with previous mistresses it held no significance. She did not mean anything to him, he assured himself. But the concern in her eyes as he had been about to walk out of the door had got to him.

He wondered if she would understand that he had felt as though his heart had been ripped out when he'd learned that he wasn't Henry's father.

His jaw clenched. How could Marnie—how could *anyone*—comprehend what it felt like to bring a child up for *six years*, to love that child more than anything else in life, and then discover from a DNA test that the boy you had believed was yours was actually another man's son?

Leandro guessed the grief he felt was similar to the pain of bereavement. He had lost his child—lost his role as a father. He'd promised Henry that they would always be friends, but nothing could alter the painful truth that the child he had cradled as a newborn baby in his arms had no biological connection to him.

Aboard his private jet, Leandro phoned Henry's headmaster and was reassured by the news that an X-ray had shown that the boy did *not* have any broken bones. Arriving in Paris, he drove straight to the hospital and was escorted to the private room where Henry was lying in bed. He was deathly pale, but managed a grin when he saw Leandro.

'Papa. My shoulder hurts.'

Leandro felt a knife blade twist in his heart. 'We decided you would call me Leo instead of Papa,' he reminded Henry gently. 'I've spoken to the doctor and he said your collarbone isn't broken, but you *have* sprained the ligaments in your shoulder. There is not a lot that can be done to treat the injury—you just have to rest it and give it time to heal. You can be discharged and I'll take you back to the apartment for the rest of the weekend, if your mother agrees.'

'Cool. Can we have pizza for dinner?'

'I'm glad your appetite hasn't been affected,' Leandro said drily.

'Maman is on holiday in Barbados, with my real father, so Monsieur Bergier phoned you. I knew you would come.' Henry's expression clouded. 'I wish you *were* my *papa*, Leo.'

The knife in Leandro's heart cut deeper. 'We'll always be best buddies. That will never change.' He rearranged Henry's pillows. 'The painkillers the nurse gave you should start working soon, so try and sleep while I go and phone your mother. I expect she is worried about you.'

'I don't suppose she is,' Henry said matter-of-factly. 'She and Dominic will be having too much of a nice time on holiday to think about me.'

'That's not true.' Leandro gritted his teeth and

forced himself to go on. 'Your mother and...and father care about you very much.'

He stepped out of the room and swore savagely beneath his breath. Nicole had told Henry six months ago that Dominic Chilton was his real father, but instead of choosing to spend time with the boy, as a family, she and her lover had gone on a month's holiday to the Caribbean.

Leandro hated feeling helpless, but he could not protect Henry from his mother's casual approach to parenting. He remembered how rejected he had felt when he was a boy and his mother had failed to turn up when she was supposed to visit him—either because she had forgotten or because she was too busy. Disappointment and hurt that neither of his parents had much time for him had been constant features of his childhood, and his concern that Henry felt the same sense of abandonment meant that Leandro had to bite back his anger when he spoke to his ex-wife.

'There's no reason for me to rush back to Paris if Henry's injury is not serious,' Nicole stated. 'Dominic and I only arrived in St Lucia a few days ago, and it's the first chance I've had to relax and enjoy a break.'

It was on the tip of Leandro's tongue to ask Nicole what she needed a break *from*, when her life consisted of shopping and beauty salon appointments. But he was bitterly aware that he had no legal rights to Henry, and that if he antagonised Nicole she could prevent him from maintaining a relationship with the boy. She would not care that Henry had declared that he wanted to stay in regular contact with 'Uncle Leandro'.

The hatred Leandro had felt for his ex-wife when he had discovered how she had deceived him had turned to contempt, and he only half listened to her whining that Dominic was facing demands for a huge divorce settlement from his wife. His thoughts strayed to Marnie, and he was struck by the contrasting characters of his ex-wife and his current mistress.

He had missed Marnie while he'd been in New York—and not only in bed, he admitted. Logically he knew he should not allow their affair to continue for much longer. A year was at least six months too long to keep a mistress. An alarm bell sounded in his mind as he acknowledged that he did not want to end the affair just yet, but he assured himself that it was because the sex was good.

Now that he was no longer so worried about Henry he was able to relax, and thinking of the passionate sex life he enjoyed with Marnie evoked an ache in his groin. He felt bad that he had hurt her feelings at the party. Would it compromise the rules he had set for their affair if he gave her a token to show that he valued her being his mistress? He frowned as he tried to think of a suitable gift. Jewellery was too emotive, and he did not want her to think that his emotions were at all involved, but flowers were too impersonal. And he usually sent flowers to his mistresses when he dumped them.

It would be useful if he knew of any hobby Marnie enjoyed, but he had no idea what she did in her spare time when she wasn't working as a cocktail waitress. She was just there in the background of his life, always cheerful and smiling as she handed him a martini when he arrived home from work, and always as eager for sex as he was at any time of the day or night. She was the perfect mistress, Leandro acknowledged.

He recalled that earlier in the summer they had spent a week cruising the French Riviera on his yacht, and one starlit night after they had made love outside on the deck Marnie had said that she liked looking at the stars. Problem solved—he would buy her a book about stargazing. A book was the sort of gift that showed he had thought about her, but not too much.

Satisfied with his reasoning, Leandro zoned back to his ex-wife's conversation. He was instantly bored but, although it irked him, he had to be diplomatic with Nicole, and it was a few more minutes before he was able to end the call and return to Henry's bedside.

CHAPTER THREE

'IT'S SUCH A shame Leandro couldn't come to the wedding. Your uncle and I were looking forward to meeting him.' Marnie's aunt, Susan, who was her mother's sister, smiled at her across the buffet table at the wedding reception. 'You said he had to dash off to Paris unexpectedly?'

'Yes, his friend was hurt in an accident but I don't know any more details,' Marnie murmured. She had hoped that Leandro would phone her, but she hadn't heard from him since he left London two days ago.

'Perhaps you and Leandro will visit when he has a free weekend?' Aunt Susan suggested. 'I'm serious about wanting to meet him. You are my sister's only daughter, and for Sheena's sake I'd like to be sure that you've met a decent man who will look after you.'

'I don't need anyone to look after me. I had

to take care of myself after Dad left, and Mum was…' Marnie grimaced. 'Well, you know how she was. Sometimes her depression was so bad that she didn't get out of bed for days on end.'

Her aunt sighed. 'I wish I'd known the extent of Sheena's mental health problems. I think she must have been devastated when she found out your father was having an affair.'

'Mum warned the twins and me that Social Services would take us into care if we told anyone about her depression.'

'Things must have been worse for Sheena after the accident. Poor Luke…twenty was far too young to die,' Aunt Susan murmured. 'Have you heard from Jake?'

Marnie shook her head. 'I last saw him about five years ago. He admitted he was taking drugs because he couldn't cope with losing Luke. He asked me for money but I didn't have any. It was a struggle to manage on Mum's welfare allowance and the small amount I earned from my part-time job while I studied for my A levels.'

Thinking about her brothers was painful, and tears stung Marnie's eyes. Growing up, she had adored the twins, who were two years older than her. They had been a happy family—especially when her father had been at home from his job as a long-distance lorry driver. But he had struggled to cope with her mother's depressive illness, and when Marnie was eleven her dad had abandoned his wife and children and stopped paying the mortgage on the family's comfortable house.

With their mother unable to work because of her depression, she, Marnie and her brothers had been moved to the estate and the twins had been drawn to the gang culture that existed there until Luke had been killed. It had been a tragic accident: he'd been thrown from the back of a motorbike that Jake had been riding.

Marnie pulled her mind back to the present as a waiter brought round a tray of sparkling wine to toast the newlyweds.

'Don't you want a glass of bubbly?' asked her uncle, Brian, when she opted for fruit juice.

'Juice is more refreshing in this heat. I seem to have gone off alcohol at the moment.'

'You haven't gone off cheese,' her uncle noted, looking at the pile of cheese and crackers on her plate. 'You're not pregnant, are you?' he teased. 'I remember Susan ate pounds of cheddar when she was expecting Gemma.'

'Brian!' Aunt Susan glared at her husband.

Marnie nibbled on a cheese straw. Thankfully an unplanned pregnancy was something she did *not* have to worry about. After years of suffering from debilitating menstrual migraines her doctor had prescribed her a type of continuous contraceptive pill which prevented her from having periods and had ended her excruciating monthly headaches.

The wedding buffet was followed by a disco in the evening, before Gemma and her new husband, Andrew, left for their honeymoon, and the guests cheered as the newlyweds drove off, trailing tin cans that someone had attached to the car's exhaust pipe.

It had been a happy family occasion, Marnie mused the following afternoon, when she boarded a train back to London. The kind of wedding she would like if she ever got married—although none of her immediate family would be at her wedding because her mother and one of her brothers were dead, and she had lost contact with her father and her other brother.

Besides which, Leandro never spoke of the future, and the subject of marriage had never been mentioned. Was it wrong of her to want to have some indication of where their relationship was heading?

She finished reading the magazine she'd bought for the train journey and picked up a newspaper that had been left on another seat. The tabloid was full of celebrity gossip, and Marnie's heart gave a sickening lurch when she flicked through the pages and saw a photo of Leandro and a stunning brunette.

She recognised the woman as Stephanie Sedoyene, a famous French model who was the current 'face' of an exclusive perfume brand. The paparazzi on both sides of the Channel stalked Miss Sedoyene relentlessly—which probably explained why she and Leandro did not look happy in the picture of them emerging from a restaurant in Paris.

Was this the Stephanie who had left a message on Leandro's phone before he had rushed off to Paris to visit an injured friend? Marnie chewed her lip. Had the story about his friend being in hospital been a cover for his dinner date with this beautiful model? In the photo, Leandro had an arm around Stephanie's shoulders, and something about their body language suggested they were comfortable with each other, as if they were old friends—or lovers.

Marnie ordered herself not to jump to conclusions. She would *not* listen to the voice in her head which taunted her, saying that Leandro was bound to find the beautiful model more attractive than a nothing-special, veering-towards-chubby waitress. But suspicion slid with the deadly menace of a poisonous snake into her mind. Maybe Leandro's regular monthly trips to Paris were so that he could visit Stephanie Sedoyene.

She closed her eyes as she was bombarded with memories from her childhood, and she heard her mother's shrill voice accusing her father. *'Who is your tart, Ray? Don't take me for a fool. I followed you when you said you were going to the pub on Friday night and I saw you and your blonde bitch going into a hotel together.'*

The idea of questioning Leandro about why a photo of him with another woman was in the newspapers was too humiliating to contemplate. She couldn't bear to sound possessive and obsessive like her mother had been. She quickly folded up the paper and put it back on the empty seat where she had found it.

But for the rest of the journey to London she could not erase the photo of Leandro and his beautiful companion from her mind, and she was deep in thought as she walked back to Eaton Square from the station.

'Marnie?'

The voice was familiar, but it was a voice from the past that she'd wondered if she would ever hear again. She spun round and saw a man walking along the pavement towards her. For a few seconds she thought she was seeing a ghost.

'Luke?' She swallowed. Of course it wasn't Luke. 'Jake! I haven't seen you for so long.'

Although it was five years since the accident, grief was still etched on Jake's thin face and he looked much older than when Marnie had last seen him.

'Where have you been for the past five years?' she said softly.

'I wish it *was* Luke here instead of me. As for where I've been…' Jake shrugged. 'Here and there, but mostly in hell.' He glanced up at the elegant townhouse. 'You seem to have done all right for yourself.'

'It's not my house. I live here with a…a friend.' Marnie flushed, but her brother shrugged.

'Hey, your life is your business, and as long as you're happy that's all that matters.'

'I *am* happy,' Marnie said truthfully. 'Leandro is a great guy. I wish you could meet him, but he's away at the moment. How did you know where to find me?'

'I went back to the Silden Estate and found it had been demolished, but I remembered you had a job at a cocktail bar on the King's Road so I went there. One of the waitresses gave me your phone number and address. I don't have a phone, since mine broke, so I came to find you.'

Jake grimaced.

'I'm sorry I haven't been around, but... Well, the truth is that I spent some time in prison after I was charged with theft. I broke into houses and sold the items I stole to buy drugs. I was in a bad place in my head after Luke died—but that's not an excuse and I'm not proud of what I did.'

'Oh, Jake.' Marnie reached out and grasped her brother's hand. 'I wish I'd been able to help.'

'In a funny way going to prison helped me, because it was hell and I never want to go back inside. I'm sorting my life out and I no longer take drugs. Tomorrow I'm catching a train up to Scotland. I've been offered a job as a grounds-man on a country estate near Loch Lomond, and I appreciate it that the owner, Lord Tannock, is giving me a chance.'

Jake looked down at Marnie's fingers, entwined with his.

'I never forgot about my little sister and I wanted to find you and make sure that you're all right.'

The lump in her throat prevented Marnie from speaking, and instead she flung her arms around her brother's neck and hugged him. 'I'm so glad to see you. Do you have a place to stay before you leave for Scotland?'

Jake shook his head. 'I spent all the money I had on a train ticket, but it's a warm night and it won't be the first time I've slept on a park bench.'

'You must stay here tonight.' It occurred to Marnie that she had never mentioned to Leandro that she had a brother, but she was sure he would not want Jake to spend the night on the streets. She called his number, wanting to check that it was okay for Jake to stay, but his phone was switched off—as it had been when she had tried to call him earlier. 'I'll try Leandro again later,' she told Jake as she led him into the house.

Jake whistled as he took in the Italian white marble floor tiles in the hallway and glanced up at the magnificent crystal chandelier. 'Wow, your boyfriend must be loaded. No wonder you're happy with him.'

'I love Leandro, and I'd love him just as much if he wasn't wealthy.'

Marnie's heart contracted as she acknowledged the depth of her feelings for Leandro. Admitting that she was in love with him made her feel vulnerable, because she had no idea how he felt about her.

She glanced at Jake and thought how difficult his life must have been since Luke had died. Grief was so hard to deal with. She had focused on her studies as a way of trying to forget the ache in her heart. It must have been even worse for Jake because he had lost his twin.

She longed to be able to help him, and an idea suddenly occurred to her. 'Grandma's pearls.'

'Sorry…' Jake looked puzzled. 'I don't follow you.'

'When Grandma Alice died she left her jewellery to her daughters. Mum had Grandma's pearl necklace and Aunt Susan was left a ruby ring. Mum didn't make a will before she took the overdose.' Marnie sighed. 'I've often wondered if she meant to take her life or if it was a cry for help. But now the necklace belongs to Mum's surviving children. I wore it recently to a party, but I want *you* to have it. I think it's worth quite a bit, and if you sell it you'll have some money to last until you get your first pay cheque at your new job.'

'Marnie, you don't have to give me the necklace,' Jake protested.

But Marnie had already entered Leandro's study and slid back a panel in the wall to reveal the safe. When she'd moved in with Leandro he had told her to put any valuable items she owned into the safe. The pearl necklace was the only piece of jewellery she possessed, and she had often wondered why her mother had refused to sell it when they had needed money.

She remembered the safe's combination and it took her only a few seconds to open the door.

'Do *all* those boxes contain jewellery?' Jake asked, staring at the numerous velvet boxes stored within the safe.

Marnie nodded, busy searching for the box containing her grandmother's pearls. 'Here it is.' She handed the box to Jake and reset the combination to lock the safe. 'Now, I'm going to cook you dinner. You're so thin—I bet you haven't eaten a proper meal for ages.'

Throughout the evening she tried to call Leandro, but his phone was still switched off. The photograph she had seen in the newspaper of Leandro and Stephanie played on her mind, but she reminded herself that her mother's obsessive love for her father had driven him into the arms of another woman.

As she undressed for bed she caught sight of her naked body in the mirror and vowed to go on a strict diet. It wasn't just her breasts that had grown bigger as a result of her gaining a few extra pounds. Her hips and bottom looked rounder and—horror of horrors—her stomach was no longer flat but had a distinct curve.

Marnie glanced guiltily at the plate of cheese and crackers she'd planned on eating for a bed-time snack. She remembered what Uncle Brian had said about her aunt developing a craving for cheese during her pregnancy. But there was no way she could be pregnant, she assured herself. She just needed to work on her willpower. Le-andro had always said he found her hourglass figure sexy, and she wished he was with her now to reassure her that her concerns about their re-lationship were groundless.

* * *

'Marnie?'

The gravelly voice infiltrated Marnie's dream and she opened her eyes, blinking in the bright sunlight streaming through the open curtains. 'Leandro?'

'You sound surprised to see me, *cara*. Didn't you get my message that I was on my way home?'

'No, I've been asleep.'

She glanced at the bedside clock and wondered why she was in bed at three-thirty in the afternoon, before the mist clouding her mind cleared and she remembered. Last night her brother had stayed at the house, but this morning when she had got up for work she'd discovered that Jake had left without saying goodbye.

Leandro threw his jacket carelessly onto a chair before he sat down on the edge of the bed. Marnie's pulse quickened as she inhaled the familiar musk of his aftershave mixed with his unique male scent. She could see the shadow of his black chest hair through his white shirt, and the dark stubble on his jaw added to his raw sex appeal.

'Why were you sleeping in the daytime? Are you ill?'

'I fainted at work.'

She recalled that she'd felt nauseous while she had been serving coffee to some customers, and when she'd returned to the kitchen she'd had the weird sensation that the floor was rushing up to meet her and suck her down into a black hole.

'The head chef thought I might be suffering from heatstroke. Maybe it's a good thing that the weather is supposed to break and a storm is forecast.'

Leandro frowned. 'I think you should see a doctor. It seems unlikely that the heat would cause you to faint. Maybe you have a vitamin deficiency.'

'Nonsense, I've got the constitution of an ox.'

She was also becoming the size of an ox, Marnie thought dismally, conscious of Leandro's gaze roaming over her body. One of the waiters at the cocktail bar had driven her home and she'd felt so tired that she'd taken off her dress

and lain down on the bed wearing only her bra
and knickers.

'You've got colour in your cheeks,' Leandro
noted, watching a rosy blush spread across her
face and neck and stain the upper slopes of her
breasts. 'But why are you wearing a bra that is
at least two sizes too small? It's no wonder you
felt faint when your breathing is restricted.'

He reached behind her and unsnapped her bra.
His grey eyes gleamed like molten silver as he
stared at Marnie's lush breasts, as inviting as
firm, ripe peaches that he longed to taste.

Leandro traced his finger over the red line on
her skin where her bra had cut into her flesh.
'Buy some new underwear with the credit card
I gave you. I enjoy seeing you wearing sexy lin-
gerie, *cara*.'

'I don't expect you to pay for my clothes,' Marnie muttered.

She was finding it hard to concentrate on their
conversation when all she could think about was
the insistent ache between her legs. She felt embarrassed that Leandro only had to look at her
and she was on fire for him. Her nipples hard-

ened and she drew a sharp breath of longing when he stroked his thumbs over the swollen tips.

Desire swept through her with the force of a tidal wave, consuming her and obliterating her uncertainty about the state of their relationship. It was more than two weeks since they had last made love and it seemed like a lifetime. She held her breath as he lowered his face closer to hers.

'Do you really feel okay?'

There was genuine concern in his voice, but also a husky sensuality that made every nerve ending on Marnie's body quiver.

'I could get you something to eat. Are you hungry?'

'Hungry for *you*.' She gave up trying to fight her weakness and gave in to her yearning to touch him, to trace the slashing lines of his hard cheekbones and run her fingers through the springy softness of his hair. 'Kiss me,' she begged.

Her words were crushed on her lips as he claimed her mouth with a possessiveness that thrilled her. *This* was where she belonged: in the strong arms of the man she loved.

'I don't think I will ever have enough of you,' Leandro said roughly. He tugged her knickers off and stared down at her naked body, his grey eyes darkening with desire.

'I've gained a couple of pounds,' Marnie muttered self-consciously, wishing she could dive beneath the duvet to hide her more rounded curves.

'Don't be ridiculous. You have a gorgeous figure.' He started to unbutton his shirt, his gaze never leaving her. 'I spent every night while I was in New York picturing you like this, ready and aroused for me, but my only source of relief was to pleasure myself.'

Marnie's pulse rocketed as Leandro stripped out of his clothes with an uncharacteristic lack of grace that for some reason moved her as much as his confession that he had missed her. The idea of him touching his own aroused body increased her desire.

He read her mind and laughed softly. 'While I was away did you touch yourself and pretend it was *my* fingers inside you rather than your own?'

Guilty colour scorched her cheeks.

Leandro stood at the end of the bed and pushed her legs apart. 'Show me,' he said hoarsely.

For a moment she hesitated, embarrassed to do something so intimate, but she trusted him and she wanted to please him—just as she knew that very soon he would use all his considerable skill as a lover to please her. Tentatively she ran her hand over the neat triangle of blonde curls at the top of her legs and stroked a finger along her moist opening.

Emboldened by the raw groan he gave, she pushed one finger inside herself and then a second digit, as she'd done when she had been alone in bed and had pretended that Leandro was pleasuring her. Through her half-closed eyes she watched his hard features tauten, giving him the look of a hungry wolf. His eyes glittered as he watched her arouse herself.

'*Dio*, I'm going to explode,' Leandro muttered.

He was tempted to watch Marnie give herself an orgasm, but his own need was too urgent. She withdrew her fingers and he positioned himself between her legs and gripped her hips as he thrust into her, deep, hard, his excitement building swiftly as she arched her pelvis towards him and accepted each stroke of his body into hers with an eagerness that he found oddly beguiling.

She was such a generous lover. He had never known any other woman decimate his control the way Marnie did. The thought set off an alarm bell inside his head. He did *not* need her, Leandro assured himself. Sex with her was amazing, but he had enjoyed great sex with other women before her and undoubtedly would have other mistresses in the future who gave him as much satisfaction as Marnie did.

Determined to prove that he was the master in their affair made him exert iron control over himself as he possessed her with hard, rhythmic strokes, thrusting into her over and over, until she gasped his name and climaxed hard, curling her fingers into his shoulders as her body shuddered with the force of her release. He waited for her to come down and then rolled her onto her stomach and thrust into her again, satisfaction surging through him when she buried her face in the pillows to muffle her cries as he drove her to another orgasm.

Only then did he permit himself to come. He threw his head back and could not restrain a harsh groan in the ecstasy of release.

Afterwards, as Marnie curled up against him and he idly stroked her hair, Leandro assured himself that his orgasm had been so intense because he had made himself wait. He had proved that what he had with Marnie was not special—it was just very good sex.

Pleased with his evaluation of their affair, he got up and strolled into the bathroom. Returning to the bedroom a few minutes later, he took a package out of his briefcase and handed it to her.

'Open it,' he instructed when she looked surprised. 'It's a present.'

Marnie's heart leapt. Had Leandro belatedly remembered their one-year anniversary? She pulled off the paper wrapping and stared at the book, titled *Stargazing for Beginners*.

'I remembered you mentioned when we were on the yacht in France that you were interested in the stars and planets, and I thought you might find the book useful,' he said casually.

Marnie tried not to feel disappointed that Leandro hadn't given her a more personal gift. A book was not very romantic, and he hadn't mentioned their anniversary, but she reminded herself that he had thoughtfully chosen a gift he believed she would like.

'The book is great, thank you,' she murmured.

She swung her legs off the bed and pulled on her robe before walking over to the dressing table and picking up her hairbrush. Her nerves felt on edge. It seemed churlish to explain to him that she had read a similar book on basic astronomy when she was fifteen, which had inspired her to gain a degree in the subject. However, she could no longer put off telling him that she had been offered an internship with NASA in America.

She took a deep breath. 'Leandro, we need to talk.'

'Mmm?' He was checking messages on his phone and gave her a brief glance. 'I expect you want to tell me about your cousin's wedding. Did it go off all right?'

'Yes, it was lovely.' Marnie allowed herself to be distracted from the conversation she needed to have with him. 'My aunt and uncle were disappointed you couldn't attend. Aunt Susan invited us to visit them in September. She offered us the use of their beach house and I thought we could stay for a long weekend.'

'Unfortunately it's impossible. I'll be in Florence for the whole of next month.'

She stared at him. 'This is the first time you've said that you will be going abroad again.'

He shrugged. 'I have a busy schedule. I can't keep you up to date on all my business trips.'

'It *is* for business, then?' She heard the sharp note of suspicion in her voice and sickeningly recognised that she sounded like her mother.

Leandro's eyes narrowed and Marnie sensed he was irritated by her questions.

'Of course my trip is for business reasons. I recently bought a derelict theatre there and I intend to oversee the renovation work.'

Leandro walked over to where Marnie was sitting in front of the dressing table and pushed aside the edge of her robe. He bent his head and traced his lips along her collar bone.

'I want you to come to Florence with me.'

Her heart leapt. 'You mean visit you while you're staying there?'

'I mean come and live at my villa with me. The house is very beautiful. As a boy I spent happy times there with my mother and grandparents.'

Those few weeks he'd spent in Florence every summer, away from his strict father and the soulless apartment in New York, were the happiest memories of his childhood, Leandro brooded. He had never taken any of his previous mistresses to the house that had such emotional ties for him, but he was confident it would not overstep the boundaries of his affair with Marnie if he took her to Villa Collina. The alternative would be for him to have to waste time at weekends travelling between Florence and London to visit her.

She looked uncertain, and he guessed the reason. 'I realise you might not be allowed to take a month off from your job at the bar, but I've been thinking that it would be better if you did not work at all. It would be convenient if you were able to travel with me.'

'Convenient?'

The word intruded on Marnie's pleasure that Leandro seemed to want to deepen their relationship and was asking her to accompany him when he went away on business trips. Her heart sank as she tried to guess how he would react to her news, and she wished she had been more open with him.

'The reason I can't go to Florence with you is not because of my waitressing job,' she blurted out. 'In fact I have already handed in my notice at the cocktail bar.'

Leandro raised his brows. 'Then what's the problem?'

'I… I've been offered a place on a postgraduate internship programme, studying astrophysics at NASA's research centre in California. It means that I'll have to live in America for the next nine months.'

CHAPTER FOUR

AS THE SILENCE stretched between them the ticking clock sounded deafening.

Leandro stared at her as if she had grown a second head. 'I'm not sure I follow you. Why would the American National Aeronautics and Space Administration be interested in a *waitress*?'

Pride bubbled inside Marnie. 'I only worked part-time at the cocktail bar. For the rest of the week I attended university in west London. I received my exam results while you were in New York and learned that I'd gained an honours degree in astrophysics.'

'Clearly congratulations are in order,' Leandro said slowly. He shrugged. 'I had no idea you were studying for a science degree. Why did you keep it a secret?'

'I wasn't at all confident that I would pass my

final exams, and if I had failed…at least only I would have known.'

She stumbled over her words, feeling shy as she revealed a part of herself that she had deliberately kept hidden from Leandro because her dream was so important to her and she was afraid that he wouldn't understand.

'Everyone I've ever told about my desire to have a career in astronomy has said that I don't stand a chance. My mother told me I should train for a "proper" job, and even the teachers at school didn't believe that I was clever enough to go to university. The school I went to wasn't renowned for producing high-achievers, and I was seen as an oddity because I was the only girl who didn't muck about in science classes.'

'I still find it odd that you withheld from me what is obviously an important part of your life.'

Marnie told herself that Leandro was not sounding hurt. How could he be when *he* had set the rules of their relationship and had discouraged any discussion about their personal lives? She had not imagined that he had always maintained an emotional distance from her.

'I'm not the only one to withhold things. You have never told me the reason for your frequent trips to Paris.'

'I don't feel obliged to give you an explanation,' he dismissed, with a cool arrogance that stirred her temper. The photo in the newspaper of him and Stephanie Sedoyene still bothered her.

'A few days ago it was the first anniversary of when we became lovers,' she said tremulously. 'Doesn't the fact that we have been together for a year give me the right to ask why you spend a weekend in Paris every month…and who with?'

The words had tumbled out before she could stop them. In her mind she heard her mother, shrilly accusing her father of being unfaithful, and she clamped her lips together to prevent herself from asking Leandro about his relationship with the French model.

'The *right*?' he said softly, dangerously. 'If you were my wife I concede that you might have the right to question me, but you are not and never will be my wife. You are my *mistress*.'

Leandro's words dropped like pebbles into

a pool, causing ripples to disturb the smooth surface. Tension knotted in the pit of Marnie's stomach. She stood up and turned to face him, conscious of her heart beating painfully hard beneath her ribs.

'I am not your mistress.'

He frowned. 'Obviously you *are* my mistress. You live for free in my house...'

'I've told you often that I believe I should move into a place of my own, but every time I viewed a flat you found fault with it and insisted I should stay with you until I found somewhere suitable.'

'I don't believe you wanted to live in *any* of those run-down bedsits you showed me.'

'I can't afford anything better. And although I don't pay you rent to live here I have always supported myself as much as possible. Admittedly I've eaten the dinners your housekeeper has prepared, but I contribute to the household expenses by buying groceries with my own money—as well as the vodka for your martinis and your favourite Russian caviar.'

'What about that designer dress you wore to the party?'

Leandro rarely bothered to check his household expenditure. He was unsettled by Marnie's assertion that she had contributed towards her living costs. His previous mistresses had been happy for him to pay for their keep, and he couldn't understand why she wanted to be different.

'I paid for the dress out of my savings, and I have always paid for my clothes and personal items with my wages from my waitressing job. I've never used the credit card you gave me. I wouldn't want to lose my independence. It would be a fundamental change in our relationship.'

'"Our relationship"?' Leandro's jaw hardened. 'We are not in a *relationship*.'

Marnie flinched, wounded by his cool tone. 'How do you explain what we have, then?'

He gave a careless shrug. 'You are my mistress and for several months we have enjoyed a sexual liaison. At some point it will run its course and we will end our affair and move on to the next chapter of our lives.'

The colour drained from her face. 'So when you asked me to go to Florence with you it was just for sex?'

'What other reason *could* there be?' He sounded bored, and a look of impatience crossed his face when he saw her stricken expression. 'I made it clear from the start, when you moved in with me, that it would not be a permanent arrangement.'

Marnie could hardly breathe for the pain in her chest as her heart splintered into a thousand shards. Leandro had casually dismantled the castle of dreams that she had built in her mind.

'The length of time you have been my mistress is immaterial,' he continued, 'and it seems that you will not fill that role for much longer anyway if you intend to accept an internship in California.'

'Are you issuing me with an ultimatum?'

Marnie realised that her knees were trembling. She felt sick, and her eyes burned with the effort of holding back tears. Only the prospect of utter humiliation if she cried in front of this coldly cynical man, who looked like the Leandro she loved but did not sound like him, kept her from breaking down.

'The placement on NASA's graduate programme is for nine months, and I very much want to go. It's an opportunity beyond anything I ever dreamed of.'

He shrugged. 'Then of course you should go.'

Her tension eased a little. It seemed that Leandro would be supportive after all. No doubt he had been initially shocked to hear that she had a science degree, and career plans beyond being a waitress, but once he'd had time to get used to the idea she hoped he would be pleased for her.

But she could not forget his harsh words. *You are not and never will be my wife.* She knew from her parents' unhappy marriage that 'wedded' and 'bliss' did not always go together, but she was devastated by Leandro's insistence that she was his mistress.

'How do you feel about me living in America for nine months?' She searched his face but found no clue to what he was thinking. 'I suppose what I'm really asking is, what will happen to us?'

'There is no *us*,' he said curtly. 'If you want to go to California—go. But I cannot see the point of a mistress who is not available all the time, and I have no intention of taking a vow of celibacy for the next nine months. So it would appear that our affair has run its course a little sooner than I'd anticipated and it will end when you leave for the States.'

The crazy thought came into Marnie's head that she would tell him she would turn down the internship. The prospect of losing him, of never again being held in his arms, was agonising. But hurt was only one of the emotions churning inside her. She felt angry with Leandro, but she was even more furious with herself—for contemplating sacrificing her career dreams for a man who had made it clear that she would never be a permanent fixture in his life.

She loved Leandro, but loving him had blinded her to the glaring truth that he did not love her. If she had needed proof that she was as pathetic as her mother, this was it. But she would not allow love to destroy her as it had her mother.

She lifted her chin and met his iron-grey gaze. 'We may as well end our affair right now, then.' She gulped as the enormity of what she was saying hit her. How could she leave him? *How could she not?* demanded a steely voice at the core of her.

She tried again to reach behind the barriers he had always held in place but she hadn't wanted to acknowledge. 'I thought…hoped…that with our having lived together for a year there might be a future for us.'

'I have never given any indication that I wanted a future with you.' Impatience was evident in Leandro's controlled movements as he pulled on his trousers and wrenched open the wardrobe to take out a clean shirt.

Marnie watched him, stunned by how swiftly her emotions had gone from happiness to despair. 'What are you doing?'

'What does it look like?' He sliced her with a rapier glance. 'It's the middle of the afternoon and I'm going back to work. We can continue this conversation this evening.'

'What's the point when there is nothing more to say?' And she was scared that she would humiliate herself by admitting she loved him.

The room had started to spin in an alarming fashion. Leandro walked over to the door and Marnie was struck by the devastating realisation that this might be the last time she saw him. But he had made it clear that she meant nothing to him and she knew she had to leave him today, or risk succumbing to her weakness for him.

Her throat felt as if she had swallowed broken glass. 'I won't be here when you get home from work. It's only three weeks until I go to California, and I can stay at my cousin's flat while Gemma is away on her honeymoon.'

'That is your prerogative.'

Leandro fought the urge to stride over to Marnie, haul her into his arms and take her back to bed, where he knew she would not resist him. He was saved from idiocy by his common sense, which reminded him that he'd had a lucky escape. When a mistress started to talk about anniversaries and the future it was time to relegate her to the past.

He saw her lips tremble and felt an odd tug in his chest. Her career ambitions were a surprise, and he wished her success with the internship in California. But he had no intention of waiting for her and he did not doubt that he would quickly replace her with a new mistress.

The thought occurred to Leandro that it was not the first time a woman had chosen her career over him. His mother had left him when he was seven years old to seek fame as a musical theatre star. But he had been a child then, and he had cried every night for months after his mother had left.

He certainly wasn't going to lose any sleep over Marnie, he assured himself. The only time he had cried as an adult was when he'd read the DNA report which had stated that Henry wasn't his son. Nothing could ever hurt as much as that. His ex-wife had brought him to his knees with her deception, but he would never allow any woman to have power over his emotions again.

He gripped the door handle and threw Marnie an indifferent glance over his shoulder.

'If you really mean to move into your cousin's place, leave your door key on the hall table on your way out.'

It felt like a bereavement—but, unlike when her brother had been killed, this time it was a part of herself that had died.

Marnie's heart had felt as heavy as lead since she had split from Leandro two weeks ago. She couldn't sleep and she had lost her appetite, and it had rubbed salt into a raw wound when she had stood on the scales that morning and discovered that she had gained another pound.

'Dr Leyton will see you now,' the receptionist told her.

Marnie walked down the corridor to the consulting room, where she had visited her GP two days ago to report the dizzy spells she'd been having as well as feeling breathless every time she climbed the three flights of stairs up to her cousin's flat. She was due to fly to California in a week's time, but before she started the intern programme she wanted to make sure she was physically fit.

Not that there was any medical solution for a broken heart, she thought as she stepped into the consulting room.

The doctor looked grave, and Marnie felt a flicker of concern. There couldn't be anything seriously wrong with her, could there?

Moments later she grabbed hold of the edge

of the desk as the GP's words sank in to her stunned brain. '*I can't be pregnant!* It must be a mistake.'

But it wasn't a mistake. The results of the blood test she'd had two days earlier showed that she was sixteen weeks pregnant, and also that she was anaemic due to an iron deficiency, which was apparently a fairly common condition in pregnancy.

'I've never forgotten to take my contraceptive pill,' she said almost pleadingly, as if the doctor could somehow change the result of the test.

'The pill is not one hundred per cent reliable, and it can be affected by certain types of antibiotics, for instance.' Dr Leyton glanced at Marnie's medical notes. 'Although you don't appear to have been ill in the past few months.'

'I had a bout of food poisoning, but the sickness only lasted for a couple of days and I didn't need medical treatment.'

'Did you use another method of contraception for the rest of the month after you were sick? The pill's effectiveness would have been reduced—especially if you vomited soon after taking it.'

Marnie remembered that in France, on Leandro's yacht, she had woken one morning and taken her pill first thing, as usual, but when she'd got out of bed she'd felt sick and had to rush to the bathroom. Leandro had insisted on calling a doctor, who had suspected that she had food poisoning after eating mussels for dinner the previous evening.

The holiday had been four months ago.

Disbelief turned to panic as the clues added up. Her weight gain and increased appetite…her tender breasts and an inexplicable urge to burst into tears—although the reason she had cried herself to sleep every night for the past two weeks had less to do with hormones and everything to do with her missing Leandro.

She tried to focus on the implications of discovering that in another few weeks she would be halfway through her pregnancy. 'I had no idea that I'd conceived and I continued to take the pill every day.'

'There is no scientific evidence that the foetus will have been affected. The next step is to arrange for you to have a scan, which will determine the exact date the baby is due.' The doctor looked intently at Marnie. 'Because you are at least sixteen weeks you will have to make a decision quickly as to whether you want to proceed with the pregnancy.'

It took a few moments for the doctor's meaning to sink in, and when it did her response was unequivocal even as she was bombarded with a hundred reasons why it was utterly impractical for her to have a baby.

'I do.'

Although she certainly had not planned to have a baby fate had decided otherwise, and she did not believe she had any option but to continue with her pregnancy. She had always known that the internship with NASA was too good to be true, Marnie thought as she realised she would have to turn down the opportunity of a lifetime. There was no way she could spend nine months at a research centre in California when she would be a mother in five months.

A mother. Dear God, she hoped she would be

a better mother than her own. Her panicky feeling escalated to full-blown fear. She had no job, no home and a pile of broken dreams for a career that was as out of reach as the planets she would have loved to study if she hadn't fallen pregnant by a man who had humiliatingly told her he only wanted her for sex.

Leandro dropped his briefcase onto the hall table on his way into the sitting room and went immediately to the bar to make himself a martini. For some reason he remembered that Marnie had said *she'd* paid for the exclusive brand of vodka he preferred in his favourite cocktail with her wages from her waitressing job.

He pictured her the last time he had seen her. She had still been flushed with a post-sex glow, but she'd been unable to disguise her hurt when he had admitted that he had never considered a future with her.

'I am not your mistress,' she had told him proudly.

Dio! He ground his teeth. She had proved to be the same as every other woman he'd been involved with and had wanted more from him than he was prepared to give. Why couldn't she have settled for what they'd had—great sex, easy companionship and no expectations of commitment?

The truth was that he missed her, and it irritated the hell out of him. It wouldn't have been so bad if he'd gone to Florence, as planned. He was sure he would have soon forgotten her. But the refurbishment work on the theatre had been delayed and he had spent the last two weeks living at his house in Eaton Square. He was reminded of Marnie every time he caught sight of her collection of potted plants on the windowsill that looked half-dead since she had left, despite the fact that he had watered them every day.

His phone rang and he smiled for the first time in days when he saw the caller's name on the screen. 'Stephanie.'

'Leandro, I'll be in London tomorrow, before flying to Ireland for a photo shoot. I want to wear some of Maman's jewellery for the modelling assignment. I can collect it in the afternoon if you will be at home.'

'Tell me which pieces you want and I'll leave them on the desk in my study in case I'm not here. My housekeeper will let you in.'

'The sapphires, and the pearl and diamond choker. Don't worry—I'll take good care of them.'

'Giulietta left her jewellery to both of us, but I'm not likely to wear it,' Leandro told his half-sister drily.

He chatted with Stephanie for a couple more minutes and at the end of the call finished his martini and decided to take the items of jewellery out of the safe while he remembered.

In the study, he slid back the panel on the wall and entered the code to open the safe. The numerous black velvet boxes contained within were labelled with a description of their contents, which made his task easier. His mother had owned a significant collection of precious gems, but a stunning sapphire necklace had been her particular favourite. Out of an idle curiosity to see again the jewels his mother had loved,

Leandro opened the lid of the box and stared at the silk lining where the necklace should have nestled.

Frowning, he searched the safe, assuming that the necklace must somehow have fallen out of the box—although he couldn't understand how. He tried to remember if Stephanie had worn the sapphires recently and perhaps put them back in the wrong box.

After a fruitless search he removed the lid of the second box he had taken from the safe and discovered that the pearl and diamond choker was also missing. With grim foreboding he checked every box in the safe and found them all empty.

What the hell...? He swore as he tried to comprehend who could have opened the safe. The only people who had access to the house were himself, Marnie when she had lived with him, and his housekeeper, Betty, who had worked for him for years. He would have sworn the housekeeper was absolutely trustworthy.

Having discounted the three people who had a set of keys to the house, he concluded that his home must have been accessed by someone else who had known the location of the safe and the combination, and also been able to deactivate the alarm system.

He raked a hand through his hair. Whoever had committed the burglary had left no evidence of a break-in, and Leandro realised it was weeks since he had last opened the safe—which meant he couldn't give the police any idea of when the theft had happened.

He phoned his security officer and instructed him to look through the CCTV footage from the cameras which were situated at the front and back of the house. 'Jim, let me know immediately if you see on film anyone loitering around outside the house. I want to gather information to give to the police.'

Later that night Leandro replayed the film clip from the CCTV camera that his security officer had alerted him to and his initial sense of shock turned to fury as he watched Marnie hugging a man before she led the distinctly unsavoury-looking character up the front steps and into the house.

It was possible that the scruffily dressed man was someone she knew from university, his rational brain reminded him. The guy looked like a hippy, which seemed to be a popular dress code among students these days.

He played the film clip again and wanted to punch something—preferably the scruffy guy's face. Marnie's tender expression as she looked at the man and then flung her arms around him suggested that the two of them shared a more intimate relationship than friendship. Leandro clenched his fists. Was the guy her lover?

There *could* be an innocent explanation for why she had invited the man into the house, but it was impossible to believe that the missing jewellery from the safe and the appearance of a stranger were not linked. There was no sign that the safe had been forced open, which meant that whoever had opened it had known the code to unlock the door.

With grim fascination Leandro watched the film of Marnie leading her friend...lover—whoever the guy was—through the front door of the house. She had known the safe's combination, and in fact must have opened the safe a few days prior to when this film had been recorded because she had worn a pearl necklace that she'd kept in the safe to the Vialli Entertainment staff party.

Leandro fast-forwarded the film and watched the scruffy guy leaving the house early the next morning. Violent anger surged through him as he was faced with proof that Marnie had invited the man to spend the night with her. In *his* house, Leandro thought furiously, with *his* mistress. *Dio*, had the pair of them slept in *his* bed? Even his ex-wife had not stooped to that level.

He poured himself another whisky, not caring that he'd already drunk half a bottle, and lifted the glass to his lips with a hand that he was startled to see was shaking with the force of his emotions. Logically he knew he should not jump to conclusions about Marnie's relationship with her hippy friend. But his usual cool logic was obliterated by a red mist of rage that he recognised with a sense of furious disbelief was jealousy.

How the hell could he feel *jealous* if Marnie meant nothing to him? Why did he want to hunt her lover down and rearrange the man's admittedly good-looking features with his fist? It was his pride that was hurt, Leandro concluded.

He ran a hand across his eyes and picked up his phone to call the police and report the jewellery theft. But it was past midnight and there was no point in calling them until the morning.

Why did he feel reluctant to tell the police of his suspicions that Marnie was implicated in the theft? If, as seemed likely, she had opened the safe for her lover to steal the jewels she deserved to rot in prison. His jaw clenched. He had *trusted* her.

He made another call to his security officer. 'Hi, Jim. Sorry it's late, but I need some information on Marnie Alice Clarke—specifically, if she has ever been in trouble with the law. Let me know if you find anything on her as soon as possible.'

There was nothing more he could do tonight,

and Leandro knew he should go to bed, but he felt too wound up to sleep. A more inviting alternative was to drink enough whisky to anaesthetise the dull ache of emptiness inside him.

CHAPTER FIVE

THE LATE SUMMER heatwave still hadn't broken, despite warnings from the weather forecasters of an imminent storm. The pavements in Eaton Square were dusty and the parched plane trees in the communal gardens drooped against the backdrop of a strangely colourless sky.

Marnie's chest felt tight as she walked up the front steps of Leandro's house. The GP had said that the breathlessness resulting from her anaemia would improve now that she had been prescribed a course of iron tablets, but as she stood on the top step and hesitated before pressing her finger on the doorbell she could feel her heart beating painfully hard beneath her ribs.

She had assumed that Leandro was in Florence, but when she'd phoned him earlier he had informed her that he was in London. To her surprise he hadn't queried her request for them to meet.

'Come to the house at one o'clock' was all he had said.

Marnie would have preferred to meet him on neutral territory, but she acknowledged that it would be better if their conversation was in private.

She was expecting the housekeeper to admit her into the house, but when the door opened she stared at Leandro. The breath rushed from her lungs as she raised her eyes to his brooding steel-grey gaze. He was casually dressed in jeans and a black polo shirt, and his dark hair was ruffled as if he had been running his fingers through it.

Marnie felt her heart break all over again. Her legs trembled beneath her and she grabbed hold of the doorframe for support.

'I thought you were going to see a doctor about these dizzy attacks you've been having,' he said as his arm shot out and curled around her waist. He half carried her into the lounge. 'Sit down before you fall down.'

Marnie rested her head against the back of the sofa and felt heartened by the concern she could see in Leandro's eyes. His face was so near to hers as he leaned over her, and she longed to close the tiny gap between them and press her lips to his sensual mouth. But they were no longer lovers and she had no right to kiss him. She had assumed she would never see him again, and the only reason she was here in his house now was because she was carrying his child.

Her stomach lurched and she abruptly sat up straight and pushed her hair back from her face. 'As a matter of fact I *have* seen a doctor, who has assured me that the dizzy spells are a symptom of a slight iron deficiency. Apparently it's quite common for women in…in my condition.'

Leandro's brows lifted. 'Your *condition*?'

'I'm…pregnant.'

It was the first time she had spoken the words aloud and they shattered the sense of unreality that had cocooned her for the past twenty-four hours.

She stared at Leandro when he laughed. 'I'm

not joking,' Marnie said tautly. 'I fail to see what's so funny.'

'Oh, *cara*, it's a hilarious joke.' His bitter tone was at odds with his laughter. 'Next you will be telling me that I'm the father.'

Marnie was glad she was sitting down, because she didn't think her legs were capable of supporting her. 'Of course you're the father. You're the only man I've ever slept with. And this…' she placed her hand on the faint swell of her stomach beneath her loosely cut cotton dress '…this is most definitely your baby.'

'Stop right there,' Leandro commanded.

His eyes were drawn to Marnie's hand, resting on what he now saw was her slightly more rounded stomach, and sheer unadulterated rage swept through him.

When she had phoned and asked to meet him he'd felt an overwhelming sense of relief that she must have had a good reason to take his mother's jewellery from the safe and obviously wanted to see him to explain. He didn't know why it crucified him to think that she was a thief, but if she intended to return the jewellery he was prepared not to involve the police.

The sight of her standing on the front step, her blonde hair tumbling in luscious waves around her shoulders and her delectable curves enhanced by a simple yet inexplicably sexy white cotton sundress, had forced him to acknowledge how much he had missed her. He'd wanted to sweep her up in his arms and carry her off to bed. After two weeks of celibacy he was desperate for sex, but annoyingly he hadn't felt at all inclined to sleep with any of the women he'd taken to dinner recently.

He let his eyes roam over Marnie. Her breasts looked fuller, and she seemed different in a way he could not define—softer, somehow, making him long to press his body against her lush curves. Maybe she *was* pregnant. But was he the father?

An image of the man she'd invited into the house flashed in his mind. 'Like hell it's my baby.'

She paled, but quickly firmed her lips to hide their betraying tremor before she stood up and faced him. For some reason the proud tilt of her chin made him feel uncomfortable.

'I don't know what reason you have for refusing to believe that you are the baby's father—'

'I'll show you the reason,' Leandro interrupted her, anger roaring through him with the ferocious heat of a forest fire as he pictured her with the hippy guy who, the evidence strongly suggested, was her lover.

'Sit down!' he barked, and felt a vicious sense of satisfaction at her startled expression. Marnie would learn that it was unwise to try to make a fool of him.

He sat down next to her on the sofa, opened his laptop, which was on the coffee table, and seconds later an image of Marnie with the scruffy guy standing on the front steps outside the house flashed onto the screen.

'Oh…' Her little gasp was barely audible, but it confirmed Leandro's suspicions that she was guilty of a gross betrayal.

'You treacherous bitch.'

The words rasped from his throat before he could prevent them, and they made him even angrier. He didn't want her to think he actually cared that she'd cheated.

'A lesson, *cara*—' he made the endearment sound like an insult '—if you want to screw around, don't do it in view of a security camera.'

He stared at her shocked face and told himself he wouldn't waste his energy on hating her because she wasn't worth it.

'How *dare* you bring your lover into my home?' he said with icy disdain as he paused the film clip on the image of the scruffy man leaving the house. 'You will see the date at the top of the screen is the day following on from when your lover arrived, which proves that he stayed the night.'

'He…he's not my lover. I can't believe you would think I'd been unfaithful,' Marnie choked. Her initial shock at Leandro's accusation gave way to anger that he could think so badly of her. 'Jake is my *brother*.'

'Sure he is,' Leandro mocked. 'It's odd that you have often spoken about your aunt and uncle who live in Norfolk, and your cousin who recently married, but you never once mentioned that you had a brother.'

'That's because I'd lost contact with Jake and I found it painful to talk about him.'

'How convenient that your long-lost brother has turned up *now*.'

'Jake *is* my brother. Why are you being so nasty?' Marnie said shakily. She felt as though Leandro was tearing her emotions to shreds. 'Jake came to see me before he went to Scotland to start a new job. I tried calling you to ask if it was okay for him to spend the night here, but your phone was switched off.'

'So, your brother…lover—I don't give a damn what he is,' Leandro sneered, 'has rushed off to Scotland? It makes sense that he would want to get away from London as quickly as possible.'

'What do you mean?'

'*Dio*—stop the pretence!' His temper exploded. 'You think I'm being *nasty*? Trust me—I'll get a whole lot nastier if you don't give me some answers. And a story about you being pregnant with my child will not lessen my anger—quite the opposite.'

'Leandro, what are you doing? You're scaring me.'

Marnie gave a cry when he gripped her arm and jerked her to her feet. He ignored her attempts to free her arm as he pulled her behind him and strode down the hallway and into his study. He halted in front of the panel on the wall, which had been moved aside to reveal the metal safe behind it.

Marnie was surprised to see that the safe door was open, and she felt a prickle of foreboding when she noticed numerous black velvet boxes, which she knew contained jewellery that had belonged to Leandro's mother, lying empty on the desk.

'Give me one good reason—other than a ridiculous tale about you being pregnant—why I shouldn't call the police and have you arrested for stealing my mother's jewellery collection?' he said savagely.

'But I didn't… I swear…'

Marnie's voice faltered as a terrible thought struck her. Could Jake have broken into the safe and taken the jewels? Of course he hadn't, she argued with herself, feeling guilty for suspecting her brother. Leandro must be the victim of a professional burglar.

'Have you looked round the house for signs of a break-in?'

'My security team have scoured the building and found nothing. They are as convinced as I am that the theft was committed by someone who had keys to the house. I didn't rob myself,' he said sardonically, 'and my housekeeper assures me that the only reason she goes into the study once a week is to do some dusting. Besides, Betty has worked for me for ten years and I don't suspect *her* of stealing the jewellery.'

'But you do suspect me?' Marnie wondered if it was possible to feel any more hurt and humiliated, but Leandro's next words showed her it was.

'You had access to the house, you knew the code to unlock the safe and six years ago you were issued with a fixed penalty notice by the police for shoplifting.'

He ignored her gasp and continued relentlessly. 'My security officer ran a criminal disclosure check on you, and although a penalty notice is not a criminal record it proves to me that you are a thief as well as a two-timing slut,' Leandro said through clenched teeth. 'It's obvious that you brought your lover to my house, opened the safe and took my mother's jewellery—which you gave to your boyfriend, presumably so that he could sell it.'

'I am not a thief!' Marnie gulped back a sob as she felt her heart splinter into a million fragments. 'The shoplifting charge was a mistake. I had picked up an expensive handbag in a shop to look at it. Then I thought I saw my brother Luke through the window and I ran outside, forgetting that I was still holding the bag.'

'I thought you said your brother's name was Jake. You need to remember your lies.'

She flushed. 'I had two brothers. Jake and Luke were twins.'

'Oh, *twin* brothers.'

His mocking disbelief felt like a whiplash on her soul and she wanted to run from his study, from his house, from *him*. She'd never, ever wanted him to know about the shoplifting charge that was the most embarrassing event in her life.

From deep inside her she dredged up what was left of her pride. 'I knew as I ran after the man I'd seen that he couldn't be Luke, because he'd died when he was twenty. But I carried on running because then I hoped it was Jake, who I lost contact with after Luke's death.' She gave a ragged sigh. 'It turned out that the man was a stranger, of similar height and colouring to my brothers, but the security guard who had chased after me from the shop refused to believe my story and accused me of stealing the handbag.'

Leandro gave a snort of impatience. 'I'm not surprised the security guy didn't believe you. I've heard enough of your lies. Either you tell me where the jewellery is or you can tell the police, who will want to know the identity of the man you brought into my house.' His eyes bored into her, hard as steel. 'Did you open the safe?'

'I...' Marnie's throat constricted.

She pictured herself entering the code to unlock the safe and taking out her grandmother's pearls. Jake had been standing behind her, and it was possible, she acknowledged painfully, that her brother had made a mental note of the eight-digit code. Jake might have stolen the jewellery, but if she admitted her suspicion to the police they would discover that her brother had already served a prison sentence for theft and it was probable that he would be sent back to jail.

Images from her childhood flashed into her mind. She had idolised her big brothers, and Jake and Luke had been protective of their younger sister. Jake had been the more daring twin, and she remembered how he had stood up to a gang of bullies at school who had made her life hell. He wasn't a bad person, but he had never come to terms with Luke's death.

'I never want to go back inside... I'm sorting my life out,' Jake had told her. If only she could talk to him and persuade him to return the jewellery—if he had indeed taken it, Marnie thought desperately. But her brother had disappeared without saying goodbye.

She lifted her eyes to Leandro's face. His hard features looked as though they had been carved from granite. He had every right to be furious, but her poor grief-stricken brother deserved one more chance. She could not betray Jake.

'*Dio*, Marnie,' Leandro swore, and then repeated his question. '*Did you open the safe?* Yes or no?'

The savagery in his voice made her flinch. The walls of the study seemed to be closing in, and the room was so hot and airless that she couldn't breathe. The sky outside the window had become ominously dark, although it was the middle of the day, and a sudden thunderclap sounded like a bomb exploding.

The shock of the storm breaking so dramatically caused Marnie's heart to pound, and with a low cry she toppled into blackness, unaware that Leandro sprang forward and caught her in his arms.

'Drink this.'

Marnie's eyelids fluttered open and it took her a few seconds to register that she was lying on the sofa in the sitting room. Leandro must have carried her here from his study, and now he was leaning over her, holding a glass to her lips.

She smelled whisky and shook her head. 'I can't drink alcohol. It might harm the baby.'

He muttered something unrepeatable as he put the whisky down on the table and handed her a glass of water. She took a few sips and rested her head against the cushions, glad that the dizziness had passed and she no longer felt as if she was riding on a carousel.

Satisfied that she was not going to faint again, Leandro abruptly moved away from her—as if he could not bear to be near her, Marnie thought miserably. She wondered who he was texting on his phone. How dare he accuse her of having a secret lover when a photo of him with a French model had been plastered on the gossip page of a newspaper?

Bitterness joined the host of other emotions swirling inside her, but she refused to humiliate herself by asking him if Stephanie Sedoyene was his mistress—especially as his answer might further break her heart, which was already in pieces.

'How did you fall pregnant?' Leandro asked harshly. 'I thought you were on the pill.'

'I am on the pill, but I forgot that it would be less effective for the rest of the month after I had food poisoning when we went to France.'

He stopped prowling around the room and strode back over to her, his heavy brows drawn together in genuine confusion. 'But that was four months ago.'

'I'm almost seventeen weeks pregnant. The type of pill I was taking prevented me from having periods, so I didn't miss a period—which is the most common sign of pregnancy—and as I didn't suffer from morning sickness I had no idea that I was pregnant.'

Leandro raked his hair back from his brow with an unsteady hand. Of all the surprises Marnie had sprung, the news that she would give birth in five months was the most astonishing. His eyes were drawn to the slight swell of her stomach beneath her thin cotton dress and his heart gave a violent leap as it occurred to him that perhaps she really was carrying his child.

His common sense immediately reminded him that he had been in this situation before, with his ex-wife. Marnie might well be pregnant, but it was possible she had been having an affair with the man she had invited to the house and her hippy lover was the baby's father.

Leandro read the text message on his phone and his jaw hardened with resolve. Marnie was still pale, but he cursed himself for feeling concerned about her. *If* the child she was carrying was his then obviously he would ensure that she had the best medical care for the rest of her pregnancy. But it was a big if.

'I want a DNA test,' he said abruptly. 'And I don't want to wait for five months until the child is born to find out if it is mine.'

Marnie swung her legs down from the sofa. Her eyes were drawn to his laptop on the coffee table and the image on the screen of her leading Jake into the house. The evidence looked bad, she admitted, especially in light of the jewellery theft from the safe, but it still hurt to realise that Leandro did not trust her.

'I promise you a DNA test is unnecessary. You must have realised I was a virgin the first time we had sex, and you're the only man I've ever slept with.'

He shrugged. 'I've learned that promises are meaningless. And if you gave away your virginity so that you could live rent-free in luxurious surroundings in Belgravia, what does that say about you?' he drawled.

The faint colour that had returned to her face drained away again, but Leandro ruthlessly ignored the inexplicable tug he felt on his heart.

'A non-invasive prenatal paternity test involves no risk to the unborn child. I have a doctor friend who owns a private practice in Harley Street, and Alex has just messaged me with the information that all that is required for the test is a blood sample from both of us. Foetal DNA found in an expectant mother's blood can be analysed and compared with DNA in the alleged father's blood. If the DNA test proves that I am the father I will accept responsibility for my child.'

'That's big of you.'

Marnie's temper simmered in response to Leandro's coldness. His curt statement that he would accept responsibility for his child should have been a relief, but he sounded so uncaring—

as if he viewed having a child as an unwanted encumbrance.

Her father had not wanted *her*, she remembered, and her mother had relied on her only to cook meals and clean the flat. Sheena's depression had meant that she'd taken little interest in any of her children.

She would love her baby, Marnie vowed, feeling fiercely protective of the fragile scrap of humanity inside her. The steel backbone she'd developed during her difficult childhood and teenage years gave her the courage to meet Leandro's cynical gaze. She would be everything her mother hadn't been, and she would love her baby twice as much to make up for Leandro's lack of interest.

'I've already told you there is no point in having a DNA test, because this baby can't be anyone's but yours. If you choose not to believe me that's your problem. But I don't expect you to take responsibility—I never expected anything from you. I simply thought you had a right to know that I am carrying your child.'

She was determined not to break down in front

of him, but when she took a step towards the door he caught hold of her arm and swung her round to face him.

'You seem to have forgotten about the missing jewellery. Perhaps the reason you are in such a hurry to leave is so that you can alert your hippy boyfriend to the fact that the theft has been discovered. You knew I rarely opened the safe and you gambled on the likelihood that I wouldn't find out the jewellery was missing until you were long gone.'

'If that was true, why would I have come to tell you I'm pregnant?' she fired back at him, incensed and deeply hurt by his accusations.

'I haven't quite worked it out yet, but it's possible your boyfriend has refused to accept responsibility for his child and has disappeared with the jewellery, leaving you with nothing, and so you've decided to try and blame *me* for your pregnancy. You were unaware that a security camera had filmed you letting your hippy guy into the house, and you believed that when the theft from the safe was eventually discovered the assumption would be that it was the work of professional housebreakers.'

'I am expecting *your* baby. If you carry out a basic check on my background and family you will discover that Jake *is* my brother.' Marnie took a deep breath. 'All right, I agree to the DNA test—which I am a hundred per cent sure will prove you are the father. And I don't know how the jewellery came to be missing from the safe.'

She couldn't be certain Jake had committed the theft and she urgently needed to talk to him.

She was pulled from her thoughts as Leandro tightened his grip on her arm and swept her out of the room and along the hallway towards the front door.

'I've arranged with Alex for us to go to his surgery immediately.'

He speared her with a lethal glance that hurt her more than anything else he had said or done.

'If I find out that you have lied and tried to pin another man's baby on me you had better make sure you hide some place where I'll never find you.'

CHAPTER SIX

AT THE PRIVATE doctors' practice in Harley Street, blood samples were taken from Marnie and Leandro. They would be sent to another clinic for DNA screening.

'I'll never forgive you for putting me through that,' she told him after they had left the surgery and were in the car, driving across west London in traffic that was heavier than usual due to the torrential rain.

He frowned. 'Did you find the blood test painful?'

'No, but I find it humiliating to have to prove that you are the baby's father when I've told you that you are the only man I've ever had sex with.'

'You have told me a lot of things that turned out to be lies. Only a fool would accept a paternity claim without proof.'

Leandro recalled that his father had said the

same thing when the truth of Henry's paternity had eventually been established. Silvestro had not minced his words.

'You should have insisted on a paternity test when the boy was born, and certainly after you divorced Nicole and agreed to pay maintenance for a kid who turned out not to be yours. You were a damned fool to wait six years before demanding a DNA test.'

Don't worry, Dad, lesson learned, Leandro thought bitterly. His father's scorn had been almost as hard to bear as his own devastation at discovering that Henry was not his son.

'You can drop me at the underground station and I'll take the Tube to Brixton. It's only a short bus ride from there to my cousin's flat in Dulwich.' Marnie interrupted Leandro's thoughts. 'It will be quicker than you driving me across town.'

'You've got to be joking. I'm not letting you out of my sight until I get the result of the paternity test in a week's time. You can stay at my house, and if it is proved that the child you are expecting is mine we will discuss how we are going to deal with the situation.'

'I'll tell you how *I'm* going to *deal* with it.' Marnie was infuriated by Leandro's superior tone. 'I'm going to be the best mother I possibly can to my baby, and I don't want or need anything from you. We have nothing to discuss, and you can go to hell for all I care.'

'I've already been there.'

Leandro flexed his hands on the steering wheel and flicked a sideways glance at Marnie. She had never lost her temper with him before, and it crossed his mind that her emotional state might not be good for the baby. If the child *was* his he would make sure that nothing upset her while she was pregnant.

He focused on the road ahead and tried not think about her voluptuous breasts, rising and falling swiftly beneath her cotton dress. If he took her to bed he could guarantee she wouldn't stay angry for long. *Dio!* He cursed beneath his breath as he felt himself harden. There was a good chance that she'd had sex with another man, he reminded himself, welcoming the cold fury that replaced his desire.

'Where do you plan to live once your cousin returns from her honeymoon? I assume you won't be going to California now.'

'Obviously I can't take up the internship with NASA this year,' Marnie said flatly, 'but there is a possibility that I can defer the placement until after the baby is born. Apparently there are excellent childcare facilities at the research centre.'

Leandro digested this unexpected news. 'Are you saying you would leave a young baby in a nursery for hours every day so that you could study? It doesn't matter how good the childcare facilities are. A baby needs to be with its parent to form a bond so that it feels secure and loved.'

His earliest memories were of being cared for by a nanny. He assumed his parents had visited him in the nursery wing of the penthouse, but he did not remember receiving much affection from his mother and father.

Marnie glanced at Leandro, startled by his emotive statement. 'That's a pretty old-fashioned viewpoint—to expect a woman to devote herself entirely to her child and maybe sacrifice her career.'

'It doesn't necessarily have to be the mother. A father can be just as good at parenting.'

When Henry had been born Leandro had been determined to be a better father than his own father had been to him. He felt a sensation as if his heart was being squeezed in a vice. If the child Marnie was carrying was his he would want to protect it. *Dio*, he would *love* his child.

'If I am the father I won't allow you to take my child to America for nine months,' he said harshly.

'You won't be able to stop me. Anyway, why would you care? You've made it clear that you don't want the baby.'

'I didn't say that. I said I wanted proof that you are expecting *my* baby, and if you are I will absolutely want to be part of my child's life.'

'Well, in that case I suppose we'll have to discuss access arrangements.' Marnie couldn't hide her surprise. 'If I join the graduate programme next year perhaps you can come to visit the baby in California.'

'How do you intend to fund your studying in America? Even if you receive an academic bursary you will still need to pay living costs. If you have to find a job as well as attend lectures you won't have much time to care for a baby.'

'I haven't worked out the details yet, but I'm sure I'll manage somehow.' Although it was difficult to see how she would be able to juggle single motherhood with studying for her career, Marnie acknowledged.

'If I am the baby's father I would be willing to pay for you to continue your studies in America, or anywhere else in the world, in return for you leaving the child with me and not contesting my claim for full custody.'

She frowned as she tried to make sense of Leandro's words. 'Are you suggesting I leave the baby behind in England with you for nine months?'

'Not just for nine months—for ever,' he said curtly. 'You would be suitably financially recompensed for giving up all your parental rights.'

Finally Marnie understood, and she felt sick. 'Do you honestly think I would give up my baby for *money*?' Her voice shook with disgust. 'What kind of man are you to suggest such a terrible thing? I don't believe *any* woman would *sell* her child as you have asked me to do.'

'It happens,' Leandro said grimly.

When his parents had divorced he'd believed that his father had been awarded custody of him by a judge. But when he was a teenager he had discovered that his mother had accepted a substantial pay-off from Silvestro Vialli in return for handing over the Vialli heir.

'I can't believe I fell in love with you,' Marnie said in a choked voice.

Leandro glanced at her and ruthlessly ignored the pull on his heart when he noticed a single tear slide down her cheek. 'I never asked you to—nor gave you any indication that I wanted you to develop feelings for me.'

'Well, don't worry, you've killed any feelings I had for you stone dead.'

'Marnie…for God's sake!'

Too late, he realised her intention as she opened the car door. The line of traffic had come to a standstill, and Leandro was powerless to prevent her from jumping out onto the pavement.

'*Marnie*—get back in the car. You need to calm down.'

He had never seen her cry before and the sight of her standing in the pouring rain with tears streaming down her face shook him.

'The only thing I need is to get away from *you*,' she yelled. 'If I could travel to Mars it still wouldn't be far enough. I hate you, and I never want to see you again.'

Leandro watched her run into an underground station and swore as the traffic began to move and he had no option but to drive off.

To say he'd handled things badly was an understatement, he acknowledged, furious with himself, because in business he had a reputation for being a brilliant negotiator. The best thing he could do now was give Marnie some space and allow her temper to cool. The fact that she had shouted at him was a measure of how badly he had upset her.

Seeing himself in this new light made him feel uncomfortable, because he recognised similarities between himself and his father. Silvestro was a control freak who expected everyone to agree with him, and as he was a billionaire it meant that people invariably did.

Leandro swore. His instinct had been to keep Marnie in his sight until he received the result of the paternity test, but she had said that she never wanted to see him again and he had to respect her wishes for now. Although if it turned out that the baby was his she would have to talk to him—either directly or through lawyers.

At least he knew where she was staying. After she had moved out of his house in Eaton Square he had phoned her once, to ask for the address of her cousin's flat so that he could redirect her mail. He refused to dwell on why every night for the past two weeks he had driven to Dulwich and parked outside the flat until he had seen Marnie turn the lights off before she went to bed. For some strange reason he slept more easily knowing that she was safe.

Marnie slept badly after her confrontation with Leandro. She was desperately hurt by his suggestion that she hand their baby over to him. He could not have a very high opinion of her—especially if he believed she had been involved in the theft of the jewellery from the safe. His unfair accusation had reminded her of when she had been arrested for shoplifting. It had been a terrible mistake. She had been so caught up in her grief over Luke's death that she hadn't been thinking properly when she'd run out of the shop holding the designer handbag.

The police hadn't believed she was innocent of stealing, but this time she was determined to clear her name and prove to Leandro that she had not stolen his mother's jewels. And the only way she could do that was to find her brother.

Jake had told her that he was going to start a new job on Lord Tannock's estate in Scotland, and when she had looked online she had found it was near to the town of Balloch, on the shores of Loch Lomond.

Her train to Glasgow left London mid-morning.

After her sleepless night Marnie was so tired that once she was settled in a seat she soon fell asleep. She was woken several hours later by the train's guard, who informed her that they had arrived at Glasgow.

'The train to Balloch leaves in five minutes from a different platform.'

'Oh, thanks.'

Disorientated from her deep sleep, and worried that she might miss her connection, Marnie grabbed her holdall from the overhead luggage rack and hurried off the train and through the busy station. But when she reached the ticket barrier in front of the platform where the Balloch train was waiting to depart panic set in as she realised she had left her handbag on the train from London.

'Damn!' she muttered as she tore back across the concourse.

She remembered she had tucked her handbag under her seat. Fearing that she would be stranded without her phone, bank cards and train ticket made her ignore the stitch in her side and run faster.

'Excuse me!' She swerved to miss colliding with a passenger who had stepped into her path.

Her feet slid from under her and she fell, hitting her head with a sickening thud on the concrete floor of the station.

Leandro checked his phone messages for the hundredth time as he walked across the terrace in the garden of his villa in Florence and lowered his tall frame onto a swing seat. Evening was his favourite time of day at the Villa Collina, but the golden sunset and the jasmine plants that covered the walls of the house with white stars and filled the air with a delicate perfume failed to ease his tension as he waited to hear from the DNA screening clinic.

He had spent the past week overseeing the renovation work on the theatre here, which he had saved from being destroyed, but the project which had once excited him no longer commanded his attention.

He reread the background report that his security team had compiled on Marnie. She had told him the truth when she'd said she had twin brothers: Luke, who had died five years ago, and Jake. What she had failed to mention was that

Jake had served one year of a two-year prison sentence for theft and had been released on probation—which meant he could immediately be sent back to prison if he reoffended.

Without a photograph to verify the identity of the man on the CCTV film, Leandro did not know if the guy Marnie had invited into his house in Eaton Square was in fact her brother, or if she had a lover. Whoever the man was, he must have stolen the jewellery—but had Marnie helped him? She had known the code to unlock the safe, Leandro thought grimly.

His thoughts turned to her insistence that she had been a virgin when they'd met. In his heart he knew it was true. He'd suspected it had been her first time, but he refused to believe that the incredible passion they had shared was in any way special.

His phone rang, and his heart slammed against his ribs when he saw the name of the DNA testing clinic flash on the screen. Taking a deep breath, he answered the call. After a short conversation he cut the connection and ran his hand across his eyes.

Santa Madre! Marnie was pregnant with his baby. He was going to be a father and, unlike Henry, this child could legitimately bear the name Vialli.

His mind flew back more than ten years, to when Henry had been born. He had not witnessed the birth, because Nicole had elected to have a Caesarean section at an exclusive private hospital, but Leandro had been allowed to visit his wife and his son—or so he'd believed then—when the baby was a few hours old.

Henry had been so tiny, so vulnerable. Leandro had never held a newborn baby before and he had been utterly smitten. Remembering the overwhelming love he had felt for Henry filled him with excitement and joy. When Marnie gave birth to his baby in a few months no one would take his child from him.

Reality intruded on his euphoria as he acknowledged how badly he had treated Marnie. Joy turned to cold dread in his heart. What if she refused to allow him to have a relationship with his child? He had proof that the baby she was carrying was his, but he couldn't cradle a slip of paper showing the result of the DNA test in his arms.

Marnie might decide to register the baby with her surname. More importantly, she might take the child to live in America, or anywhere in the world, and he would be powerless to stop her. He was almost certain that he would not win a custody battle, and the prospect of having only visitation rights and spending alternate birthdays and Christmases with his child was unbearable.

His jaw clenched as it occurred to him that Marnie was unlikely to remain single for ever. She was young and beautiful and there was every chance that she would fall in love with some other guy. If she married, another man would become *his* child's stepfather.

Leandro rubbed the bridge of his nose. His heart was beating hard and fast in his chest. The only certain way that he could have full legal parental rights over his baby was if he married Marnie. He had vowed never to marry again, but he was prepared to do whatever was necessary to claim his child.

But there was a problem with his plan. The last

time he had seen Marnie she had told him she hated him and she'd sounded as if she meant it. He accepted that she had every right to be furious with him because he had doubted the baby was his, and perhaps she was still angry—she hadn't answered any of his calls during the past week. But somehow he would have to convince her that they must put their child's interests first.

There was no reason why they couldn't have a successful marriage. Without the emotional expectations that most marriages carried they could focus on building a relationship based on friendship and a desire to be good parents. Their sexual compatibility was another factor in their favour.

He pictured Marnie the last time they had made love, when he'd arrived home from Paris after visiting Henry in hospital. She had looked so beautiful, lying naked on the bed with her blonde hair spread over the pillows. She'd smiled at him and he'd felt an odd sensation in his chest, as if a hand had squeezed his heart. Of course all he felt for her was sexual desire, he assured himself. But sex was as good a base as any other for marriage.

Leandro preferred action over inactivity, and he decided that his first move would be to buy an engagement ring for Marnie. She had loved him once and he was confident he could persuade her to forgive him. What woman, he asked himself, would be able to resist a diamond ring and a marriage proposal from a multi-millionaire who was determined to make her his wife?

'Leandro, thank heavens you're home.'

His housekeeper, Betty, greeted him when he walked into his house the next morning, after an early flight from Florence.

'The police have been here and they want to talk to you urgently. They say that Marnie is in hospital.'

Time froze. A lead weight dropped into Leandro's stomach.

'*Hospital?* Why? What's happened? Is she ill…has she been in accident?'

Had she lost the baby?

It stuck him as strange that he had thought

of Marnie first and the baby second. But he did not dwell on the anomaly as he called the number that the police had given to his housekeeper.

The news was shocking. Marnie had been found unconscious at a Glasgow railway station. Witnesses reported that she had been running along the platform when she had tripped and fallen. The police officer told him that she had been unconscious for two days and had not been carrying any form of identification. When Marnie had finally regained consciousness she had asked the police to contact Leandro.

The officer had no more information about Marnie's state of health and cold fear gripped Leandro as he tried to guess what effect a serious fall that had left Marnie in a coma for two days might have had on her unborn baby. He would watch over her like a hawk for the rest of her pregnancy, he vowed.

He called his pilot and within the hour was on his private jet bound for Scotland. Although he fired up his laptop he could not concentrate on work. Had Marnie gone to Scotland to warn her brother, Jake—or whoever the man on the CCTV film was—that the jewellery theft had been discovered?

Leandro remembered that the last time he had seen Marnie she had been so determined to get away from him that she had leapt out of his car while they had been in a traffic jam. The memory of her standing in the rain with tears streaming down her face made his gut clench. He was puzzled that she had asked the police to contact him rather than her relatives in Norfolk.

At the hospital in Glasgow he was directed to a side room adjoining a main ward.

'Miss Clarke will be pleased to see you,' a nurse told him. 'Her aunt and uncle, who are her next of kin, have been informed of her accident, but she insisted that you were contacted first.'

Leandro was puzzled by what the nurse had said. He thought it was unlikely that Marnie would give him a warm welcome, but to his surprise and relief she greeted him with a smile when he stepped into her room. It was a good sign that she was sitting up in bed, but she was deathly pale.

'Leandro! Oh, thank goodness I remember you.'

'*Cara*, thank God you're all right.'

Emotions that Leandro had not expected to feel surged through him as he scrutinised the livid purple bruise on Marnie's brow. He strode over to the bed and carefully drew her into his arms. Her hair smelled of lemons and felt like silk against his cheek. He closed his eyes, over-whelmed for a few moments. He had forgotten how small she was. She seemed so fragile.

His eyes were drawn to the gentle swell of her stomach, visible beneath her hospital gown, and he swallowed hard. 'The baby...?'

'I had an ultrasound scan this morning, which showed that the baby is fine.' She drew away from him and her mouth wobbled. 'I couldn't be-lieve it when the doctor told me I'm expecting a baby. I have no recollection of being pregnant— just as I don't remember a lot of other things.'

He frowned. 'What do you mean?'

Tears slid down Marnie's cheeks. She looked utterly wretched and scared, Leandro realised. Tension seized him. She wasn't making any sense.

Hiding his concern, he sat on the edge of the bed and took her cold hands in his. 'Try to be calm, *cara*...'

'How can I be calm?' she sobbed. 'Leandro... *I've lost my memory.*'

CHAPTER SEVEN

'THE DOCTOR SAYS I have retrograde amnesia, which sometimes happens after a brain injury,' Marnie explained, wiping away her tears with the tissue Leandro had handed her. 'Apparently I banged my head so hard when I fell that I cracked my skull. I've had a brain scan, which shows some swelling. It should get better, and the brain trauma specialist I saw said that my memory might improve, but there's no guarantee that it will come back.'

Leandro was aware of his heart beating hard and fast. Marnie had been through a terrible ordeal and it was vital that he did not upset her further, he told himself. If she did not remember being pregnant then it followed that she had no recollection that they had parted acrimoniously, with anger and mistrust on both sides.

'What is the last thing you remember?' he asked gently.

She rubbed her brow. 'I know that I have been living with you at your house for a few months. You asked me out to dinner and we ended up in bed together.' A tinge of colour stained her white cheeks.

He nodded. 'We became lovers and you moved into my house a year ago.'

'That long?' she said wonderingly. 'I remember we stayed in a chalet in some mountains. It must have been last Christmas. You were going to teach me to ski, but we spent most of the week snuggled up in front of a roaring fire...' Her flush deepened.

'Making love for hours.' He finished her sentence.

'If we've been having a relationship for a year I suppose we must be happy together?' Marnie didn't know why a little niggle of doubt in her mind prompted her to ask the question.

Leandro smiled. 'Of course we are happy, *cara*.'

'It's just that I don't remember a lot about *us*. I

know you work long hours, and I've been busy studying for my degree.' She looked at him questioningly. 'You *do* know that I go to university and study astrophysics? I don't remember when I told you about my dream of one day being an astronomer.' She sighed. 'It's strange that I can recall everything I learned in my lectures, but I don't know if I passed my final exams.'

'You gained a first-class honours degree.'

'Did I?' Her face lit up. 'How wonderful!'

Leandro waited for Marnie to talk about the offer she had received of a placement on the internship programme with NASA, but she did not mention it and neither did he. There was no point in confusing matters even more by reminding her that she had planned to spend nine months studying in California. He would not allow her to take the baby to the other side of the world and leave it in childcare for hours while she pursued her career dreams. He was determined that his child would feel loved and secure—unlike the way he had felt when he was growing up.

He pulled his mind back to what Marnie was saying.

'I assume I had intended to carry on studying for my masters at the same university in west London, but I don't remember the plans I made.' Her voice cracked. 'What's worse is that I don't remember finding out that I'm pregnant.'

She bit her lip.

'I'm guessing my pregnancy was an accident? It's not something I would have planned at this stage of my life.' She put her hand on the slight swell of her stomach. 'But it's quite exciting to think that our baby will be born in a few months. Are you pleased that you're going to be a father?'

Leandro let out a controlled breath. 'I'm over the moon, *cara*. Your pregnancy was only confirmed a few weeks ago and, yes, it was a surprise, but I couldn't be happier.'

'I'm so glad. I wasn't sure how you felt.' She visibly relaxed and her smile lit up her face.

Leandro ruthlessly ignored the tug on his conscience. He was a gambler, he reminded himself. He had made his multi-million-pound fortune by taking risks that other men did not have the guts to take. Gambling on Marnie's memory loss being permanent was crazy, even for him, but he was willing to do anything to claim his child.

'I can't wait for our baby to be born,' he assured her. 'But before we become parents we have another special event to look forward to.'

He reached into his jacket pocket and took out a small velvet box bearing the name of the jewellers in Florence where he'd bought the ring before returning to London.

Marnie gave a little gasp when he opened the lid to reveal a stunning diamond the size of a small rock.

'I had your engagement ring resized,' Leandro told her smoothly as he lifted her hand and slid the ring onto her finger. 'Good—it now fits you perfectly.'

He looked into her stunned eyes and dismissed the irritating voice that said it was wrong of him to trick her into marriage.

'I think we should carry on with the wedding plans we made before you lost your memory.'

'Wedding plans! That means you must have proposed. I'm so sorry, but I don't remember.'

Her mouth trembled and Leandro felt his gut twist, but he ignored the pang his conscience gave.

'Try not to get upset,' he said soothingly. 'We will make new memories—starting now. Will you marry me, *mia bella*?'

Marnie stared at the huge diamond sparkling on her finger and wondered why she didn't feel ecstatic, the way a bride-to-be should. Leandro was waiting for her to respond, and she felt guilty that this must be almost as difficult for him as it was for her.

She gave him a strained smile. 'Of course my answer is yes. But are you sure you want to marry me? What if my memory never returns?'

'Perhaps it will over time.'

Leandro knew it was selfish of him to hope she would not remember his recent behaviour. If she regained her memory he would face a far harder task to convince her to marry him.

He lifted her hand and pressed his lips to her fingers. He would make her happy, he assured his conscience. While she had been his mistress she had fallen in love with him without any effort on his part.

Fate had worked in his favour, and Marnie did not remember that he had demanded a DNA test to prove the baby was his. He saw no point in reminding her. All he had to do was convince her that their marriage was a love match and she would never guess that he was marrying her for the sake of convenience.

'As soon as you are fit enough to be discharged from hospital we will go to my villa in Florence, so that you can recuperate and be ready for our wedding in a month's time.'

Marnie's brow pleated as she tried to remember the plans that she and Leandro had presumably discussed for their wedding day, but the fog obscuring her memory would not budge. It felt so strange that she was effectively missing several months out of her life. It was as if there was a veil drawn across her mind. Every so often she had a tiny glimpse of the past, but frustratingly the snatch of memory always faded.

One thing she was certain of was that she had fallen in love with him within the first month of moving in with him. She'd thought about him all day while she was working at the cocktail bar or attending lectures at university, and felt like a lovesick teenager as she'd waited for him to come home from work. Sometimes they hadn't even made it out of the hall and had made love up against the wall. She blushed at the memory of their mutual and very urgent desire for each other.

And Leandro must have fallen in love with her as he had asked her to be his wife. The engagement ring on her finger felt unfamiliar, but he had said that the ring had needed to be resized, so perhaps she had not had a chance to wear it.

A flicker of uncertainty made her say, 'Perhaps we should postpone getting married until my memory comes back?'

She wondered if it was her imagination that he suddenly seemed tense. But then he gave her a sexy smile that made her toes curl. He was so gorgeous, and his grey eyes were as soft as woodsmoke as he held her gaze. Her indefinable doubts disappeared and all she could think of was how incredibly handsome he was.

'You have to accept that you might not regain your memory,' he said gently. 'Our baby is due in a few months, and it means a lot to me that our son or daughter will be legitimate and have parents who have made the commitment of marriage. I want us to be a family and I thought you shared my feelings.'

'I do,' Marnie whispered, deeply moved by his words. She loved the thought of being part of a family with Leandro and their baby. Her own childhood had not been particularly happy after her father had left, and she wanted her baby to grow up feeling safe and secure.

Tiredness swept over her, and she closed her eyes as the headache that had been a permanent feature since she had regained consciousness became a throbbing pain.

'You're right. We should carry on with our wedding plans even though I can't remember what those plans are. I don't want my stupid accident to spoil things, but I might have to leave the arrangements to you.'

'I'll take care of everything, *cara*.'

Satisfied that stage one of his plan to make

Marnie his wife as soon as possible was under-way, Leandro was impatient to submit the nec-essary paperwork which would allow them to marry in a minimum of twenty-eight days.

An unfamiliar emotion that was perhaps ten-derness swept over him as he watched her eye-lashes drift down and fan on her cheeks. He wanted to wrap her up in cotton wool. But his concern was for his child, he reminded himself.

Believing that she was asleep, he walked noise-lessly over to the door, but as he was about to step out into the corridor her voice halted him.

'Leandro, do you love me?'

'Why else would I have asked you to be my wife?' he murmured after a slight hesitation. 'Rest now, *cara*, and I will talk to the consul-tant and find out when you will be well enough to fly to Florence.'

It had not been the most romantic declaration.

Marnie blinked away the tears that inexpli-cably filled her eyes as she watched Leandro walk out of the room and shut the door behind him. She wished he had kissed her, or said that he loved her with more enthusiasm than he had demonstrated. But perhaps he had been told by the medical staff not to overexcite her. She certainly did not feel overwhelmed by his visit, she thought ruefully.

The brain trauma specialist had explained that it was common to feel emotional following a head injury, and she told herself that was probably the reason she wanted to cry. It was a horrible feeling to have a great big gap in her memory and, although she hadn't said so to Leandro, he seemed more like a stranger than a loving fiancé.

She held up her hand and studied the huge diamond on her finger. Leandro must love her because he had asked her to marry him. But she could not dismiss the sense that there were undercurrents between them she did not understand.

As she rolled onto her side she felt a strange fluttering sensation in her stomach. Holding her breath, she placed her hand on her belly and felt a faint but distinct movement. Her baby! One of the nurses had explained that expectant mothers were usually able to feel their baby move at about four and a half months pregnant. Suddenly her pregnancy seemed much more real. A new life was developing inside her and the prospect of motherhood was miraculous and daunting.

She wondered how Leandro had reacted when she had told him she was expecting his child. Why did she think that he had been angry? He seemed pleased now, and she told herself that once she had got over the shock of discovering that she was soon going to be a mother she would relax.

But as she rested her aching head against the pillows she felt very alone, and afraid of what the future might hold.

The Villa Collina was located on a hill above Florence and the view from the terrace over the historical city and surrounding Tuscan landscape was breathtaking.

'Have I been here before?' Marnie asked Leandro. 'I can't believe I wouldn't remember such a beautiful place.'

She could not hide her frustration that nearly two weeks after she had been knocked unconscious her memory hadn't returned.

'This is our first visit to Florence together,' he reassured her. 'You must try to stop worrying about your memory loss. Stress isn't good for the baby.'

'You don't know what it's like to have months of your life obliterated from your memory.'

Marnie sighed as she looked around the villa's gardens, where manicured lawns were bordered by late-flowering lavender bushes that filled the air with a heavenly scent. The only sound to disturb the still air was the low drone of bees, but even the tranquillity of the surroundings did not give her a sense of peace.

She had hoped that if she went back to his house in London it might trigger her memory, but Leandro was keen to return to his work on a theatre restoration project in Florence and he had persuaded her to fly out to Italy with him and stay at his villa, so that he could keep a close eye on her.

She could not fault his attentiveness, she acknowledged. He constantly fussed about her health, and of course she was glad that he was taking such an interest in her pregnancy, but sometimes she wondered if his concern was more for the baby than for her.

Pushing away the uncharitable thought, she turned her head to study him. When he had visited her every day in the hospital he had looked gorgeous, wearing a three-piece suit, and Marnie had found it irritating that all the nurses had sent him admiring looks. Today he looked ruggedly sexy, dressed in hip-hugging jeans and a light blue denim shirt. His dark hair was ruffled by the breeze and the golden afternoon sunlight accentuated the angular beauty of his face.

Marnie thought it was amazing that a man as handsome and sophisticated as Leandro had chosen her to be his wife.

'I feel that I don't *know* you,' she burst out. 'I suppose you must have told me about your family, for instance, but I don't remember.' She looked towards the elegant three-storey villa. 'Why did you buy this house in Florence? Were you born in this part of Italy?'

'As a matter of fact we've never really talked about our respective families.' Leandro realised that he would have to open up about himself a little more as Marnie was going to be his wife. 'I was born and grew up in New York. My paternal grandfather had moved to the States from Naples and established a property development business there. When he died my father took over the company and built Vialli Holdings into a billion-dollar business.'

Marnie frowned with the effort of trying to force her mind to see into the past. 'I don't remember if I have met your parents.'

'My mother is dead, and my father rarely socialises unless it is for business reasons,' Leandro said shortly.

He led Marnie into the villa, where pale grey Italian marble floors and whitewashed walls offered a cool sanctuary from the sun-drenched garden.

'My mother grew up in this house. My parents divorced when I was seven and I lived with my father, but I spent holidays here with my grandparents, and occasionally with Giulietta if she wasn't working on a show.'

Something jolted in Marnie's mind. 'Oh, your mother was Giulietta Fargo—the famous singer and Broadway legend.' She felt a rush of excitement when Leandro gave a nod of affirmation. 'I don't know why I remember that, but the fact that I do must be a good sign that I'm starting to regain my memory.'

Leandro's reaction was more cautious. 'My mother was an international star—most people have heard of her. The specialist warned you it could take months, maybe years, for you to regain your memory, and it might never come back. His advice was for you to get on with your life.'

He caught hold of her hand and led her through the villa.

'Come and see the rest of the house.'

Marnie was enchanted with the villa's homely feel. Colourful rugs on the floors and paintings of Tuscan scenery on the walls lent charm to the elegant rooms.

Walking up the wide staircase, she paused to look at a photo on the landing of a boy of about ten years old and a woman with long black hair. 'Is that your mother? She was very beautiful.

Why did you live with your father after your parents split up?'

'My mother's career meant that she was constantly travelling around the world. I didn't actually see her very often. She tried to be here when I visited my grandparents, but her stage performances always came first.'

There was no bitterness in his voice, simply a flat note of resignation, but Marnie's tender heart ached as she studied the photo of Leandro as a boy and saw loneliness and a haunting vulnerability in his grey eyes.

'Who is the little girl?' she asked, indicating the toddler in the photo.

'My half-sister. After my parents divorced, my mother had an affair with a French businessman, which resulted in a daughter. In the same way that she had left me to be brought up by my father, she left Stephanie in the care of *her* father. When we were children I only met her occasionally, when my mother brought her to Villa Collina, but after Stephanie's father died a couple of years ago we became closer.'

Leandro picked up another photo of a stunningly beautiful young woman. 'This was taken of Stephanie last year. She's a successful model based in Paris.'

Stephanie. Marnie had no idea why she felt a reaction to the name. 'Have you spoken about your half-sister before?' she asked Leandro.

'Possibly not. Like I said, we didn't tend to talk about our families.' There was an odd note in his voice when he went on. 'I only found out fairly recently that you had brothers who were twins, and that one of them had died.'

'Luke's death is one memory I wish I *could* forget.' Marnie sighed. 'For a long time after he was killed I couldn't accept that I would never see him again. Once, I even…'

'What?' Leandro prompted.

'Oh, there was a terrible incident when I was in a shop and I thought I saw Luke outside the window. I ran after him, not realising that I was still holding a handbag that I'd picked up. Of course it looked like I was trying to steal the bag, and I was arrested, but it was a genuine mistake. I miss both my brothers so much.'

Marnie put down the photo of Leandro and his

mother, and the one of his half-sister, thinking that his childhood did not sound much happier than hers had been.

'My dad left when I was eleven and moved to Bulgaria to be with a woman he had met there,' she explained. 'At first he used to phone me, but after a while he stopped calling and I'm no longer in contact with him. I will *never* live apart from my child,' she said fiercely.

Talking about the past had made her think about her worries for the future.

'I hope we're doing the right thing by getting married. My memory loss makes it feel like we're almost strangers,' she admitted.

She twisted her engagement ring round on her finger.

'This ring, for instance. It's the biggest diamond I've ever seen, and it must be worth a fortune, but it's not *me*.' She struggled to explain what she meant. 'I don't think I would have chosen such a flashy ring. I'm not interested in statement jewellery.'

She bit her lip as it occurred to her that Leandro might have chosen the ring for her.

'I don't mean to sound ungrateful. I suppose what I'm actually worried about is…can we make our marriage work if I never regain my memory?'

Silently Leandro acknowledged that their marriage was more likely to succeed if Marnie remained in ignorance of the accusations he had thrown at her before he'd had proof that she was carrying his child.

He sought to reassure her. 'Of course our marriage will work, *cara.*'

Her doubtful expression warned him that it would take more than words to convince her. He was also aware that if her memory returned at any time after they were married there was a chance she would leave him and try to take their child.

Although he would be in a stronger legal position with regard to winning a custody battle, he had no wish to put his child through the trauma of a divorce—he remembered what it had been like when *his* parents had split up. He wanted his child to grow up with a loving, attentive mother—as Marnie had vowed she would be.

Therefore he needed their marriage to work… which meant he must make Marnie believe that he was in love with her.

He led the way down the hall and into the master bedroom. He noted the soft colour that flared on her cheeks as her eyes darted towards the bed.

'I admit your engagement ring is extravagant. It's a male thing,' he said with wry amusement. 'Size matters to a man when he chooses a ring that he hopes will demonstrate the depth of his feelings for the woman who has agreed to be his wife. But I should have known that you would prefer a ring with less bling.'

He remembered that when she had been his mistress she had never shown any interest in designer clothes or expensive jewellery. Her tastes had been for simpler things, such as the daffodils he had picked from the garden in the spring and given to her.

'You chose a beautiful ring for me,' she said huskily. 'I didn't mean to hurt your feelings.'

'You could never do that, *cara*.'

Leandro's words were designed to reassure

her, but silently he assured himself that Marnie could not hurt him because he felt nothing for her. Although that was not quite true. He felt desire. Hot, hungry desire that burned in his gut and made him ache more than he had ached for any other woman.

He was glad to see that she was no longer deathly pale, and the bruising on her temple had almost disappeared. While she had been a patient at the private London hospital, where he had arranged for her to be transferred from Scotland, his focus had been on making sure she received good medical care. But now he noticed the glossy sheen of her honey-blonde hair and the soft pink colour on her cheeks before he moved his eyes down to her round, ripe breasts.

He had always appreciated her hourglass figure, and the fuller curves that were a sign of her advancing pregnancy had a predictable effect on his body. The silky material of her dress was stretched across her tummy, and he longed to place his hand on the proud swell where his child lay. He imagined pulling her dress down and stroking his hands over her abundant breasts, and desire ripped through him.

He smoothed her hair back from her face. 'You have had a busy day…it would be a good idea for you to lie down on the bed for an hour or so before dinner,' he murmured.

'I'm not tired. I'm feeling much better now my headache has finally gone,' she assured him.

'In that case I think we should both lie down, *cara*.'

'Oh…' Marnie caught her breath when she saw the glint in Leandro's eyes and his meaning became clear.

Relief mingled with the delicious tingle of excitement that swept through her. While she had been in hospital following her accident he had been kind and caring, but he had seemed more brotherly than lover-like, and his gentle affection when he'd kissed her cheek had made her wonder if he still desired her.

He bent his head and captured her mouth in a sensual kiss that turned to something deeper and darker and left her in no doubt that he wanted her as desperately as she wanted him. She lifted her hands and touched his face, tracing her fingertips over the hard ridges of his cheekbones and the firm line of his jaw. The rough stubble that shaded his jaw felt wonderfully familiar, and her heart lifted as she realised that she *knew* him, had touched him like this before. The evocative scent of his aftershave teased her memory and his kiss stole her heart.

'We are not strangers, *mia bella.* Your body recognises mine and remembers the passion that blazed between us from the first time we met.'

Leandro pulled her into the hard strength of his powerful body and Marnie stopped worrying that she could not remember the past and focused entirely on the present. Her breasts felt heavy, and she sighed with pleasure when Leandro freed them from her too-tight dress. It occurred to her that soon she would have to buy some maternity clothes for her expanding figure—but then Leandro took off her bra and stroked his thumb pads over her ultrasensitive nipples and her thoughts scattered as sensation arrowed down from her breasts to her hot, molten core.

Her worry that he might find her pregnant shape unattractive dissolved when he tugged her dress over her hips and slid her knickers down.

'Bellissima,' he said hoarsely. 'I have missed you so much, *mia amata.'*

He kissed her again with a fierce hunger that thrilled her, but his words niggled in her mind.

'Why did you miss me? I thought we had been living together before I had my accident.'

She wondered if she imagined the sudden tension in him.

'I missed you when you were in hospital,' he murmured.

And before she could say anything else he captured her mouth again in a sizzling kiss that made her forget everything but what he was doing with his hands as he roamed them over her body. He sank onto his knees in front of her and traced his lips over the gentle curve of her belly.

'I felt the baby move again this morning. It's just a little flutter inside me, but as the baby grows bigger you might be able to feel him or her kick when you place your hand on my stomach…if you want to, that is.'

Leandro had said he was pleased about the baby, but he'd admitted that her pregnancy was not planned and she didn't really know how he felt.

'I want to be involved in every stage of your pregnancy.' Leandro's voice was husky with desire and a tenderness that he had never felt before. He stood up, and his expression was suddenly serious. 'Do you feel well enough for me to make love to you? If you are at all worried about the baby…'

'The baby will be fine,' she said quickly. 'Before I was discharged from hospital the doctor said that I should try to lead a normal life and that it is perfectly okay to have sex for as long as I want to.' She unfastened his shirt buttons and ran her hands through the dark hair that grew on his chest. 'I want you so much.'

'I'll be gentle, *cara*,' he promised as he lifted her and laid her on the bed.

Marnie watched him strip off his jeans and boxers and the sight of his rock-hard erection caused molten heat to pool between her legs. She spread her legs wide as he positioned himself over her. But he made her wait, and made her desperate with need when he lowered his head and tormented one taut nipple and then the other with his tongue while he slipped his hand between her thighs and aroused her even more with his clever fingers.

Marnie arched her hips as drove her to the edge and held her there. 'Please,' she moaned. 'I don't want you to be gentle.'

He growled something in Italian as he pressed forward so that the tip of his erection pressed against her moist opening. Slowly, so slowly that she wanted to scream, he thrust into her, inch by inch, filling her, possessing her, and claiming her body, her heart and her soul.

She remembered *this*. As he withdrew almost fully and sank into her again, a little deeper, a little harder, she dug her fingers into the bunched muscles of his shoulders and urged him to move faster, faster, taking them both towards ecstasy.

Her heart said he was the love of her life, but something held her back from saying the words

I love you out loud. Instead she whispered them against his throat as he thrust the deepest yet and they came simultaneously, panting and groaning in the pulsing pleasure of release.

Afterwards he smoothed her hair back from her face and kissed her lingeringly on her mouth. But he did not say the words she longed to hear, and when he moved away from her it felt as if the distance between them was much wider than a few inches of mattress.

Her eyes prickled and she turned her head away from him, but she was not quick enough to hide her overspilling emotions.

'Tears, *cara*?' His voice roughened. '*Dio*, did I hurt you?'

'No.' Marnie ignored the pain in her heart. 'I just hate not being able to remember so many details of our relationship.' She bit her lip. 'If we were happy together why did I go to Scotland alone? I have no idea why I was at the train station in Glasgow.'

'You were going to see your brother Jake,' Leandro said after a moment. 'He visited you in London before he went to Scotland to start a new job.' He looked at her intently. 'Do you remember anything about your brother's visit to Eaton Square?'

'Jake came to see me?' More tears filled Marnie's eyes. 'Oh, I wish I could remember.' She caught the glint of the diamond ring on her finger. 'I suppose I went to Scotland to tell Jake that I'd got engaged. At least I will see him at our wedding. You *have* invited him to the wedding, haven't you?'

'We'd planned on a very small, intimate service, with just the two of us and a couple of friends as witnesses.' Silently Leandro acknowledged his frustration that his security team had not managed to locate Jake Clarke or the missing jewellery.

Marnie frowned. 'I'm sure I would have decided on a small wedding, but I would *never* have agreed to be married without inviting Aunt Susan and Uncle Brian and my cousin Gemma and her fiancé. Apart from Jake, they are the only family I have left, and my aunt will want to see me in my wedding dress.' Marnie noticed a flicker of surprise on Leandro's features. 'You will have to help my memory. Have I already chosen a wedding dress? It would be odd if I haven't, seeing as the wedding is in one month.'

'You decided to wait and choose a dress nearer to the date of the wedding, because you didn't know what size you would be,' Leandro quickly fabricated a reason for the delay while he made a mental note to invite Marnie's relatives to the hotel in London where he had booked a simple wedding service. It was important that Marnie believed he genuinely wanted to marry her—which he did, he assured himself.

His conscience stirred. When he had seen the CCTV footage of her inviting a man into the house in Eaton Square he'd suspected that she had opened the safe to allow the guy who was possibly her lover to steal the jewellery. But Marnie had insisted that she knew nothing about the theft, and he was starting to wonder if she might be innocent of the crime—just as she had told him the shoplifting charge soon after her brother's death had been a mistake.

It also seemed likely that the man *was* her brother Jake and not her lover. He had DNA proof that the child she was carrying was his, Leandro brooded, and before he'd seen that film he had never had a reason to think she was unfaithful. But if he revealed that he had accused her of cheating and stealing she would very likely refuse to marry him.

He could see no alternative but to go ahead with the wedding he had arranged in England for next month and pray that Marnie never regained her memory of how he had treated her.

CHAPTER EIGHT

'WHAT MADE YOU interested in restoring old theatres?' Marnie asked Leandro one afternoon, a week or so after they had arrived in Florence. They were sitting in Piazzale Michelangelo, a famous square which offered panoramic views over the city. From the cafeteria where they were drinking latte they could see the iconic terracotta tiled roof of the Duomo.

Earlier in the day they had visited the Teatro Musicale, a beautiful eighteenth-century theatre that had become derelict until Leandro had bought it with the intention of restoring it to its former glory.

'Money,' he said bluntly. He grinned at her surprised expression. 'Forget any notion you might have that I save ancient buildings out of a romantic love of history. I'm a businessman, and

I only restore theatres that I'm certain I can turn into profitable venues.'

She looked at him thoughtfully. 'I'm not sure that's entirely true. I watched you walk around that theatre that you are paying to be restored and it was obvious that you have a genuine love of old buildings.'

'I certainly admire great architectural design.' Leandro paused and then said ruefully, 'I'll admit that the Teatro Musicale has special meaning for me because it's where my mother started out as an opera singer before she went on to become a world-famous star of musical theatre.'

'What was your mother like? She was such a big star. I've seen the film versions of a couple of musicals she starred in and her voice was amazing.'

'Giulietta was incredibly talented. She had a presence both on stage and off it, and she drew people to her. She had the ability to make people fall in love with her just by smiling at them—including me.'

He laughed, but Marnie heard pain in his voice when he spoke again.

'I was fascinated by her, and when I was a boy I longed to be with her so that she would smile at me and make me feel like she loved me. But I'm not sure that my mother actually loved anyone other than herself.'

'Children need to feel loved,' Marnie said fiercely. 'My mother suffered from a severe depression, which meant that she was unable to care for me and my brothers. Sometimes I used to think it was my fault that she was so unhappy. I was a very well-behaved child because I thought if I was good my mum might stop crying and my dad might come back to live with us again.'

She had spent her life trying to please other people, Marnie realised, and the result was that she lacked self-confidence.

'I want our child to grow up feeling secure and knowing that we will love him or her unconditionally,' she told Leandro.

'That's what I want too, *cara*.'

He gave her one of his heart-stopping smiles

and the fleeting doubts that she sometimes felt about their relationship melted away.

As they strolled across the piazza Marnie was aware that Leandro attracted the attention of every female he passed. It wasn't surprising when he looked like a film star, dressed in black jeans, a polo shirt and designer shades, she conceded. What *did* surprise her was why a gorgeous hunk like him had chosen to marry someone as unglamorous and ordinary as her.

'Why are you frowning?' he asked, catching sight of her expression. 'Are you tired of sightseeing? Maybe we should go home so that you can lie down and rest.'

She giggled. 'I spend a lot of time lying down, but not necessarily resting.' Marnie caught her breath when he took off his sunglasses and she saw the wicked gleam in his eyes. 'Can we go back to that market stall close to Ponte Vecchio which sells those adorable baby clothes?'

'Of course—but, seriously, if you feel tired we'll stop at a gelateria and you can have another ice cream.'

'I'm going to be the size of a house if I keep eating so much,' Marnie said ruefully.

'Nonsense, *mia bella*, you look gorgeous. Pregnancy suits you.'

She darted a glance at him, sure he was teasing, and found him looking at her with an indefinable expression in his eyes. Time stood still and the noises of the crowded street faded.

'I wish my memory would come back,' she said, frustrated.

'The future is what's important, not the past,' he murmured. 'Let's look forward to our life together as man and wife and as parents.'

A group of teenagers ran past them, talking loudly, and the spell was broken. What the hell had happened to him? Leandro asked himself as he guided Marnie through the market place. It wasn't like him to talk about his feelings regarding his mother, but Marnie was a good listener and he had found himself opening up to her in a way he had never done with other women.

Her childhood sounded grim, and then she had suffered the tragedy of her brother's death, but there was no bitterness in her. She was kind and compassionate and his conscience pricked. It was unfair to rush her into marriage when he had not been completely honest about his reason for wanting to make her his wife. But he would make her happy, he assured himself. She would never guess that he had married her just to claim his child.

They found the stall where Marnie had bought a few gorgeous baby outfits on a previous trip to the market. This time she bought a delicate knitted shawl—'Because the baby will be born in the winter,' she reminded Leandro.

They strolled along the Ponte Vecchio, the famous bridge that spanned the River Arno, and on the way back to where they had parked the car Marnie stopped to buy a bottle of water from a shop. She frowned as she counted the money in her purse.

'The market seller on the stall where I bought the shawl gave me five euros too much change. I didn't notice at the time. I'll have to go back and return the money.'

'It's only five euros—which is probably the amount the stall owner overcharged you for the shawl. The prices are always higher for the tourists,' Leandro said drily. 'It's too far for you to walk all the way back to the market, *cara*.'

But Marnie was already retracing her steps back to the bridge. 'Five euros might not seem a lot to a millionaire,' she told him, 'but it's not my money and I'm going to give it back. You don't need to come too. Why don't you wait in that café until I come back?'

Leandro slipped his arm around her waist. 'Of course I'll come with you. But after all this walking you and I are going to have a long siesta this afternoon,' he promised.

As they walked back to the market he brooded on whether someone who was worried about repaying five euros was likely to be a thief. Everything pointed to Marnie being scrupulously honest, and it simply did not seem likely that she had stolen the jewellery. But had she been protecting her brother? Now, of course, her memory loss meant that Marnie was unaware of the jewellery theft.

Guilt tugged on Leandro's conscience as he remembered how she had wept when he had accused her of being a thief. What if he had been wrong? *Dio*, he hoped she didn't regain her memory, because he did *not* look good, he acknowledged uncomfortably.

The weather continued to be fine as late summer slipped into early autumn and the leaves on the trees started to turn to gold. It was warm enough to eat dinner out on the terrace most evenings, and there was no breeze to stir the flames on the candles that formed a pretty centrepiece on the table.

'How did you become interested in astronomy?' Leandro asked one night. He was admiring the way Marnie's hair gleamed like pure gold in the glow of the candles. She seemed to grow more beautiful with every day, he mused. Her pregnancy gave her body a lush softness that was utterly sensual and he frankly could not have enough of her.

Marnie tipped her head back and looked up at the night sky, where the silver disc of the moon was suspended against a backdrop of black velvet and a hundred, thousand, million diamond-bright stars studded the firmament.

'When I was a kid my dad used to take me and my brothers camping in the summer, and at night when it was dark we would try and count all the stars.' She smiled. 'Sometimes when I look at the night sky I think about Dad. He has another family in Bulgaria now, and I wonder if he takes his children camping and tells them about the stars.'

Leandro ordered himself to resist the tug on his heart. 'I'm sorry your father left you.'

'I missed him a lot, and I think I studied obsessively as a way of forgetting about all the problems at home. The universe is so vast, and it kind of puts all the things that human beings worry about into perspective.'

Marnie walked further down the garden, away from the light spilling onto the terrace from the house.

'Mind you don't fall into the pool,' Leandro warned as he strode after her. 'Even with a bright moon, the garden is almost pitch-black. I'll switch on the outside lights.'

'No—don't. You can see the stars more clearly without any light pollution.' Marnie tilted her face up and spotted many of the constellations that were like familiar friends to her. 'I always hoped to work as a scientist for the European Space Agency one day, but I guess I'll have to delay those plans while the baby is young.'

She felt a pang of regret for the dreams she'd once had. Although she was excited about the baby, the prospect of motherhood was daunting—not least because neither of her parents had been great role models.

'Are you close to *your* father?' It was odd that Leandro rarely mentioned his father. 'You said you were brought up by him after your mother left.'

'I was brought up by a series of nannies and childcare experts with specialist knowledge of whatever behaviour traits I demonstrated at various stages of my youth and my father wanted removed from the Vialli heir.'

Leandro's tone was ironic, but Marnie visualised the boy in the photo that she glanced at every time she walked along the landing in the villa, and she remembered the loneliness in his eyes. 'It doesn't sound as though your father was very loving,' she commented.

'Silvestro loves two things—money and power. He did not seek to have custody of me so that we could bond as father and son...he wanted to control me. We fought many battles, and, no, there wasn't—and isn't—a lot of love between us.'

Love had also been lacking in his first marriage, Leandro brooded. After he had discovered how Nicole had betrayed him by letting him believe that Henry was his son he had sealed up his emotions and locked his heart away where no one would find it.

Not even a woman with hair the colour of golden honey and tawny brown eyes that darkened with desire. *Especially* not her, he thought grimly.

He breathed in the scent of jasmine and told himself it was from the plants that grew in profusion over the pergola. But he could not resist stepping closer to Marnie and he felt his gut twist when he inhaled the sweet jasmine fragrance of her skin.

She came into his arms with a willingness that would have stirred his conscience if he'd had one. But he had set out to charm her when he had brought her to Florence and he knew, in the way he always knew with women, that he had succeeded.

She told him so in the softness of her lips beneath his when he kissed her, and in her sighs of delight when he pleasured her with his fingers and pressed his mouth to the hot, tight core of her femininity. He knew she loved him because she breathed the words against his throat as she bucked and writhed while he thrust into her molten fire, holding back from his own orgasm until she had climaxed once, twice, and her keening cries told him he had charmed her utterly.

In truth he had found it easy to make her happy. She asked for nothing except the enjoyment of his company when he took her sightseeing in Florence. Because he loved the city he had enjoyed taking her to the Duomo and the Uffizi Gallery, to admire incredible works of art by Michelangelo and da Vinci, and they had strolled across the iconic Ponte Vecchio hand in hand just like all the other pairs of lovers.

Leandro had found himself being charmed by her good humour and her surprisingly dry wit, and without realising it he had relaxed his iron guard on his emotions as together they'd explored the city and the surrounding countryside. And the places that he had known from the holidays he had spent in Florence as a boy seemed bright and new because Marnie was with him.

The moonlight glimmered on the swimming pool and cast a gentle gleam on a sun lounger as he lowered her carefully down onto it, before kneeling over her and seeking her mouth with his. He kissed her deep and slow beneath the canopy of stars, and when he undressed her in the moon shadow and ran his hands over the bountiful curves of her breasts and stomach he felt a curious ache inside him that he assured himself must be desire—because he did not feel anything else for her.

He had taught her well, and when she stroked her soft hands over his naked body, drew his hard shaft into her mouth to tease and torment him, he shuddered and tangled his fingers into her silky hair to tug her head up.

'Witch.' He groaned as she gracefully lifted herself over him and slowly absorbed his powerful erection inside her velvet heat.

Lying on his back, with Marnie straddling him, her long hair falling forward onto his chest, Leandro stared up at the bejewelled heavens. 'It's likely it was on another starlit night that you conceived our child, when we made love on the deck of my yacht in France.'

The moment he had spoken he regretted making a comment that would direct Marnie's mind to the past, but the damage was done.

Marnie was so focused on the exquisite sensation of being stretched and filled by Leandro's awesome arousal that for once she did not try to force her mind to remember. But his words evoked a wisp of memory, as fleeting and fragile as the fluttering of a butterfly's wings: a boat, moonlight, the smell of the sea carried on a gentle breeze… The images disappeared but left her with hope.

'I think I remembered—just for a few seconds. But that's a good sign that my memory will return.'

Afterwards she wondered if she had imagined that Leandro's smile had seemed to become strained. But he gave her no time to think as he rolled her beneath him and urged her to wrap her legs around his back, allowing him to deepen penetration.

'It doesn't matter, *cara*. Nothing matters but this.'

He thrust hard, and she gasped as her body welcomed his mastery.

'The past isn't important. While we've been in Florence we have made new memories, and we must look to the future...when our child will be born.'

He began to move with a devastating rhythm that drove everything from Marnie's mind but her need to reach the highest peak, and she sobbed his name as he held her there, teetering on the brink, before he let her fall into the intense pleasure of an orgasm that made her body tremble and her heart sing.

Her only regret was that Leandro still had not

told her he loved her, and she had held back from saying the words to him. But she was sure he cared for her. He had been so attentive and charming—so *loving* since he had brought her to Florence.

She told herself it wasn't surprising that he found it hard to express his feelings. He had felt unloved by his father and had been abandoned by his mother when he was a boy. Perhaps he would say the words she longed to hear after they were married. She wasn't going to let a tiny shadow spoil her happiness and excitement for the wedding that was now only a week away.

Everything was perfect, she reiterated to herself later, when they went back to the villa and Leandro insisted on carrying her upstairs to their bedroom as if she was as delicate as spun glass rather than a woman who was visibly five and a half months pregnant.

She fell asleep in his arms, but during the night she was disturbed by unsettling dreams—or were they memories buried deep in her subconscious? And the next morning she woke to a curious feeling of foreboding that the happy times she had shared with Leandro while they had been staying at the villa had all been a dream, and reality was an ominous cloud on the horizon.

A week later they flew back to London on Leandro's private jet, and the reality of her forthcoming life as the wife of a multi-millionaire was brought home to Marnie in a number of ways.

The plane was out-of-this-world luxurious, and the two stewardesses in attendance during the flight were incredibly elegant. Marnie felt horribly aware of her expanded figure and wished she had worn something less eye-catching than the brightly coloured sundress which had been fine to wear around the villa, but fell short in the sophistication stakes.

Leandro had tried to persuade her to buy new clothes for her pregnancy, but she felt uncomfortable using his credit card and the couple of dresses she had bought she'd paid for with her own money.

At least her wedding dress was stunning. She felt a ripple of excitement as she pictured the ivory silk gown which was cleverly cut to skim over her baby bump and decorated with tiny crystals that sparkled like stars on the bodice and the lace overlay of the skirt.

She turned her head towards Leandro, who was sitting beside her, and her stomach dipped as she studied his hard-boned profile. He was clean-shaven today, and his strong jaw and sharply defined cheekbones were as beautifully sculpted as the marble statues in the Uffizi Gallery. For the first time in a month he was formally dressed, in a dark grey suit and a crisp white shirt, and he looked heart-stoppingly handsome and rather formidable.

'Stop staring at me.' He laughed when she blushed. 'If you keep looking at me like you want to eat me I'll wish the flight was longer and there was time for me to show you the plane's bedroom.'

Marnie wished she wasn't so obvious. Leandro knew he had her wrapped around his little finger, but she was unable to stop herself from falling more in love with him every day.

'I need you to sign some paperwork before

the wedding.' He slid a sheaf of printed papers across the marble-topped table. 'I'm sorry there are so many pages. My lawyers are meticulous about every detail.'

'Details of what?' A lead weight dropped into Marnie's stomach as she read the document's heading. 'Do we really need a prenuptial agreement?'

'It makes sense. I am a wealthy man in my own right, and I am my father's only heir. It is my duty to protect Vialli Holdings' billion-dollar assets.'

Beneath Leandro's casual tone was a harder note that reminded Marnie of his reputation as a ruthless businessman.

'I would *never* want money from your father or from you if we broke up,' she said curtly, struggling to hide her deep hurt. 'It doesn't seem very optimistic to discuss our divorce before we are even married.'

'It's just a formality. Once you have signed the prenup we can put it away and forget about it,' he murmured, in the soothing voice that Marnie was beginning to recognise he used when he was determined to get his own way. 'Read through it later, when you are at the hotel, and you will see that it is simply to protect both our interests.'

A stewardess came to offer coffee and some irresistible little pastries. As Marnie bit into a sugary treat she brooded on how convenient it was that the stewardess had arrived with a distraction just when Leandro had needed it.

The pilot's voice sounded over the intercom, asking them to fasten their seat belts as the jet prepared to land in London. Her heart lifted as she looked forward to seeing her aunt and uncle.

'It was a lovely idea of yours to arrange for me and Aunt Susan to have a day of spa treatments at the hotel before you and Uncle Brian join us for a pre-wedding dinner tonight.'

'I'm afraid I've had to change my plans and I won't be having dinner with you. When we land, in a few minutes, my chauffeur will drive you to the hotel to meet your relatives while I fly to Paris. I will be back tomorrow morning.'

Marnie could not hide her disappointment.

'Why do you have to rush off to Paris the day before our wedding?'

'Business,' Leandro said briefly. His thoughts turned to Henry, and the latest bombshell that his ex-wife had dropped when she had phoned him the previous evening.

Dominic and I plan to make a fresh start in Australia, now that his divorce has been finalised. Obviously Dominic is keen that our son will come and live in Perth with us, and it will be a chance for Henry to get to know his father,' Nicole had said.

Leandro had resisted commenting on the fact that Dominic Chilton's desire to be a father to his son had been far from obvious for the first ten years of Henry's life. And if Chilton was committed to building a relationship with his son, Leandro accepted that it would be best for the boy. He was going to Paris to say goodbye to Henry before he emigrated.

We will still be best buddies, he had assured Henry in a text. But in reality Leandro knew he must encourage Henry to settle quickly into his new life in Australia with his real father.

* * *

The wedding was to take place at an exclusive hotel overlooking Hyde Park, but Marnie's excitement was dimmed when she arrived in the limousine without Leandro. His chauffeur escorted her into the elegant lobby.

She felt more cheerful when she spotted her aunt, stepping out of the lift.

'You look wonderful. Pregnancy suits you,' Aunt Susan greeted her.

Marnie invited her up to the honeymoon suite, and both women's jaws dropped as they admired the opulent white and gold décor, the velvet carpets, and the magnificent chandeliers hanging from the ceiling.

'What a shame that Leandro has had to dash off to Paris,' Aunt Susan said. 'I remember he couldn't come to Gemma's wedding because he went to Paris to visit a friend who had been hurt in an accident.'

'I don't remember Gemma's wedding…'

Marnie felt her usual sense of frustration about her memory loss. But her aunt's comment had evoked something in her mind. Like a flashbulb going off inside her head, she visualised a train and a newspaper lying on the seat. What an odd thing to remember, she thought. Why would a newspaper be significant?

'Are you feeling all right? You've turned very pale.' Aunt Susan looked anxious.

'I'm fine. I've just got a bit of a headache. I think we might have a storm later.' Marnie glanced out of the window at the sullen grey clouds scudding across the sky. Autumn had turned the leaves on the trees in Hyde Park to shades of red, orange and gold, and they fluttered from the branches like colourful confetti in the wind. 'I hope it doesn't rain tomorrow for the wedding.'

'It will be perfect, whatever the weather,' her aunt reassured her. 'I must admit that your uncle and I were surprised when Leandro phoned only a couple of weeks ago and told us you were getting married. Everything has happened so quickly. But I suppose you couldn't delay the wedding...' She looked pointedly at Marnie's rounded stomach. 'I hope you aren't rushing into things, dear.' Aunt Susan was suddenly serious.

'You don't *have* to marry Leandro because you are pregnant.'

'I'm not. I love Leandro and he…he loves me.'

'Well, that's all right, then.' Aunt Susan smiled.

Marnie tried to dismiss her doubts, but they and her headache lingered all day, and even a massage and pampering session in the hotel spa did not help her to relax.

That night, alone in the huge bed in the honeymoon suite, she assured herself that she was doing the right thing by marrying Leandro, and that of course he must love her. *But he had never actually told her he did*, whispered a little voice in her head.

She wished he was with her now, but he had told her he would spend the night before their wedding at his Belgravia house. When she had said she would rather stay with him, and perhaps going back to the house might trigger her memory to return, he had quipped that it was supposedly bad luck for the bride and groom to see each other just before the wedding.

It was odd, but Marnie had almost believed that he did not *want* her to visit the house where she had lived with him for a year, most of which had been obliterated from her mind.

But he wasn't staying at the house in Eaton Square tonight because he had gone to Paris. For business, he'd said. And Aunt Susan had reminded her that Leandro had missed her cousin Gemma's wedding because he'd been in Paris.

In the distance came the low rumble of thunder. Marnie shivered as something stirred in her mind. There had been a thunderstorm—when? She screwed up her face as she tried to remember. Why did she have a vague recollection of a storm and torrential rain? Why could she see herself in Leandro's study in the house in Eaton Square? Most oddly of all, why did she feel a sense of dread when she imagined marrying him tomorrow—today, she amended when she glanced at the clock and saw that it was three a.m. and she was still awake.

Her headache was preventing her from sleeping, but the storm *and* her headache would both be gone by morning, she told herself.

But she was wrong. The storm was about to break and wreak havoc.

CHAPTER NINE

LEANDRO SWORE AS he struggled to knot his tie with fingers that were as useful as a set of thumbs. All bridegrooms felt tense on their wedding day, he told himself. Hell, he should know. This was his second attempt at marriage, after all. But he had been a lot younger when he'd married Nicole: greener and much less cynical. He had believed he was in love with her, which proved what a gullible idiot he'd been at twenty-four.

Over a decade later he had no illusions that love was a fool's game he had no intention of playing.

His brief trip to Paris to visit Henry had been painful when the time had come to say goodbye.

'You'll come and see me in Australia, won't you, Leandro? Mum says you will be welcome to stay at our new house,' Henry had said with

heartbreaking innocence. *'My real father has promised that he and I will learn to surf, and as you can already surf we could go to the beach together—the three of us.'*

'Hey, buddy, you're going to have such a good time with your father.'

Leandro pictured Henry, all skinny legs and huge eyes, and drew a ragged breath that hurt his chest. He would always be there for Henry, but the boy now had a father who was finally showing an interest in him.

On his early-morning flight back from Paris Leandro had reminded himself that soon Marnie would give birth to his baby, and before that he would make her his wife. This time nothing and no one would take his child from him.

Finally satisfied with his tie, he picked up his jacket and opened his bedroom door when he heard a knock.

'I'm sorry to disturb you, Leandro,' his housekeeper, Betty, said. 'But there's a man here asking to see you.'

'Did he give a name?'

'Jake Clarke. He says he's Marnie's brother.

I explained that she isn't here, and that you're busy, but…' Betty trailed off as Leandro strode along the hallway.

'Where is he?'

'I showed him into the sitting room.'

The man who stood up from the sofa was even scruffier than he had looked on the CCTV film. 'Mr Clarke.' Leandro kept his tone unemotional, but the hand by his side clenched into a fist that he was seriously tempted to connect with Marnie's brother's jaw.

'I'm looking for Marnie.' Jake's face was gaunt, and he pushed his unkempt hair out of eyes that were dark and haunted. 'The woman who let me in said that my sister isn't here. I need to see her.' He swallowed convulsively. 'I need to return these to her.'

He opened his rucksack and tipped a pile of jewellery onto the coffee table. Leandro immediately recognised the sapphire necklace that had been his mother's favourite.

'Marnie was so sweet when she insisted on giving me the pearl necklace that had belonged to our grandmother—which makes what I did even worse,' Jake said hoarsely. 'I stole jewellery that I guess were gifts from you to Marnie. When I saw all those velvet boxes in the safe I went a little crazy. I told myself that the jewellery was probably insured. I'd watched her open the safe and I remembered the code.'

Jake groaned.

'My God, what kind of man steals from his own sister? You look disgusted—and I'm disgusted with myself. I've carried the jewellery around for weeks. I knew I had to return it. Every single piece is there,' he told Leandro, 'as well as my grandmother's pearls. I want Marnie to have them back.'

'Give me one good reason why I shouldn't report you to the police,' Leandro said harshly.

'I assumed you already had. You have every right to call them now and have me arrested. It's what I deserve. You have no idea how much I despise myself.'

Leandro had a fairly good idea of how Jake was feeling. His own feelings of self-hatred swirled like acrid poison in his gut. *Dio*, the truth had hit him like a hammer blow. Marnie was completely innocent. While they had been in Florence he had begun to doubt that she had stolen the jewellery, but now Jake had confirmed that she'd had nothing to do with the theft.

Deep in his heart he hadn't needed confirmation, Leandro acknowledged grimly. He had known that Marnie was not guilty of any of the terrible accusations he had thrown at her. But he had ruthlessly taken advantage of her memory loss to trick her into marrying him because he had told himself that he deserved to have his child.

Deserved. He almost laughed out loud at his arrogance. What he 'deserved' was to rot in hell.

He glanced at her brother. 'Marnie wouldn't want you to go back to prison. Get out of here and go and sort your life out.'

After Jake had gone, Leandro poured himself a whisky and noticed with savage contempt that his hand was shaking. He wiped beads of sweat from his brow, yet inside he felt frozen. Everything was slipping out of his control and he didn't know what to do.

How could he go ahead with the wedding and marry Marnie knowing that it was a lie—all a lie? She believed that he loved her—and she loved him. He knew she did because she was intrinsically honest, and she wouldn't have agreed to marry him unless she loved him.

He took a gulp of the whisky and dragged in a deep breath while he tried to collect his thoughts. Marnie didn't remember the accusations he had made against her, and her memory had not shown any real signs of returning. He was almost home and dry.

Once she was his wife he would take absolute care of her. He was rich and she would want for nothing. It occurred to him that Marnie wanted very little. She wasn't materialistic. But, goddammit, they could have a *good* marriage—he knew he could make her happy. And nothing altered the fact that he wanted his child.

He told himself that the stinging sensation at the back of his throat must be from the whisky. He needed this baby to ease the ache in his heart. And perhaps, whispered a little voice in his head, he needed Marnie too.

* * *

'Has Leandro arrived yet?' Marnie looked at the clock for the hundredth time. 'The wedding ceremony is booked for two o'clock and it's five to. He's cutting it very fine.'

'He's probably caught in traffic. Your uncle heard on the radio that roadworks are causing major disruption in west London. I'm sure he'll be here any minute,' Aunt Susan tried to reassure her. 'You look beautiful, my dear. Your dress is exquisite, and no one would guess you are nearly six months pregnant.'

Marnie glanced at her reflection in the mirror and conceded that her dress *was* a fairytale gown and her hair and make-up *did* look good, thanks to the stylist who had arrived at her suite at eight in the morning to help her get ready.

But the headache which had begun in the middle of the night was still pounding, and it hadn't helped that the stylist had spent an hour tugging and pulling her hair into an elaborate up-do. Another hour had been spent having her face made up and her nails painted a pretty shade of rose pink. Now Marnie's headache was excruciating, and she felt nauseous and dizzy.

Aunt Susan was standing by the window. 'That must be Leandro getting out of his car. At least the man is wearing a corsage, so I assume he's the bridegroom. I'm looking forward to finally meeting your elusive husband-to-be at the wedding.' Her smile faded when she noticed Marnie's drawn face. 'You're very pale. Are you feeling unwell?'

'Just pre-wedding nerves.'

Marnie could not explain to herself why she felt so on edge. She loved Leandro, she reminded herself. He had been a faultlessly attentive fiancé for the whole month they had spent at his villa in Florence, he'd arranged to have their wedding at this stunning venue and tomorrow they would fly to the Seychelles for a ten-day honeymoon at a five-star resort.

Everything was wonderful. It was just a nuisance that her head felt as if it was going to explode.

Leandro was met by his half-sister on the front steps of the hotel.

'Where have you *been*?' Stephanie demanded

after she had greeted him in her inimitable French style by kissing him twice on both his cheeks. 'I was starting to panic that you would be late.'

'The traffic was murder.'

Leandro did not reveal that he had spent so long arguing with his conscience about whether to go ahead with the wedding that his chauffeur had had to break the speed limit on the way to the hotel.

He raked his hair back from his brow with an unsteady hand. 'I'm here with two minutes to spare. Let's get inside. There's going to be one hell of a storm.'

Marnie jumped when there was a knock on the door of the honeymoon suite and Uncle Brian walked in.

He gave her a cheery smile. 'Ready, lass?'

'I think so.'

Her heart was thumping as she picked up her bridal bouquet of white roses and followed her uncle out of the room. Together with her aunt they walked along the corridor to the head of a sweeping staircase that led down to the wedding room on the floor below. Over the top of the banister rail Marnie glimpsed their guests, sitting down on white chairs decorated with pink ribbons, waiting for the ceremony to start.

Uncle Brian squeezed her ice-cold hand and chatted to her in an attempt to ease her nerves. 'It's lucky you didn't decide to have the wedding in a marquee. Listen to that rain. The storm is worse than the one we had last night.'

The pain in her head was unbearable. Lightning flashed outside the window and it felt as though it had burned her eyes. Gritting her teeth, Marnie held on tightly to her uncle's arm and put her foot on the first stair. Looking down, she could see a blur of faces. Then her vision cleared and she saw Leandro, more handsome than ever in a light grey suit, navy blue shirt and grey silk tie.

The woman standing beside him seemed vaguely familiar. She was tall and slender and had a mass of dark brown hair. Of course…the woman was Leandro's half-sister—Stephanie. Marnie remembered there had been a photo of the beautiful French model at the Villa Collina. But where had she seen a different photo of Stephanie?

A wisp of a memory came into her mind and she saw a newspaper photo of Leandro and his half-sister. *But when she had seen the photo she hadn't known that Stephanie was Leandro's half-sister.*

The sudden thunderclap was deafeningly loud, and it shook the glass in the windows. Images flashed into Marnie's mind like a series of snapshots—neon bright and starkly revealing.

She had been on a train, and when she had seen the picture of Leandro and a beautiful woman in a newspaper she had felt sick with jealousy that the woman was Leandro's lover. It didn't make sense. *Why* hadn't she known that the woman was his half-sister? *Why* had she mistrusted him if they had been in a happy relationship as he had told her?

'Oh...' Marnie lifted her hand to her head, as if she could somehow stop the waves of pain that kept coming—*bang, bang*—like gunshots being fired into her skull. Every explosion of white light revealed another picture—and un-covered another memory.

'Marnie, are you all right, *cara*?' Leandro's voice was sharply urgent as he moved towards the bottom of the staircase and looked up at her. 'What's wrong? Do you feel faint?'

What's wrong?

Oh, God, was she going mad? The memories bombarding her brain couldn't be true…they were too awful…but she knew they *were* true, and the pain in her heart was even more terrible than the pain in her head.

She let go of her uncle's arm and walked down a few stairs so that she stood at eye level with Leandro. It felt strange not to be looking up at him. And how she *had* looked up to him, she thought bitterly. She had put him on a pedestal and allowed him to treat her very badly.

'You can stop the pretence of being a caring fiancé. I've regained my memory, Leandro, and I remember *everything*.'

She did not imagine that he paled.

'Marnie…'

He reached out his hand towards her but she

jerked away from him before he could touch her. Below her in the wedding room she was aware of the shocked expressions on their guests' faces. The tense silence was only broken by the ferocious lashing of the rain against the windows.

'You refused to believe the baby was yours and insisted on a prenatal paternity test,' she said, her voice shaking with emotion.

Behind her she heard Aunt Susan gasp.

Leandro's face was taut and strained. 'I know I am the father. I have had the result of the test.'

'Is that supposed to make me feel better?' Marnie's throat ached, but she could not cry yet. She would not let him see her fall apart. She had suffered enough humiliation at Leandro's hands to last her a lifetime. 'You accused me of stealing the jewellery that had belonged to your mother.'

Leandro's lips were bloodless. 'I know you didn't break into the safe. I know it was your brother. Jake returned the jewellery this morning.'

'So all this time you've believed I was a thief?' She swallowed a sob. 'After my accident why did you pretend that we were already engaged and let me believe that we had begun to plan our wedding?'

She felt the baby inside her move, and gave a raw laugh as understanding dawned.

'Of course—you wanted your child. I remember now. You told me that if the DNA test proved it was your baby you would want to be involved. But you wanted more than to share custody of our child—*didn't* you?'

Trembling with the pain in her head and the pain of her breaking heart, she forced herself to go on.

'You offered me money to hand our child over to you. My God, Leandro, you were willing to *buy* my baby. That's *monstrous.'*

Outside the rain had lessened, and inside the wedding room a stunned silence held everyone in its thrall. Leandro looked as if he had been carved from granite and his skin seemed stretched tightly over his hard-boned features.

'Let me try to explain.'

Marnie shook her head and Leandro saw the horrified disgust in her eyes. He made another jerky movement towards her. His jaw clenched when she shrank from him.

'Whatever happened in the past, we were happy in Florence,' he said urgently. 'You remember I made you happy.'

That was when Marnie realised the extent of his cruelty, and nothing could have prepared her for the agony of feeling as though he had stabbed her through her heart.

'Was it all fake? When you held my hand as you showed me your favourite places in Florence? When you picked an orange from the tree in the garden and peeled it for my breakfast every morning?' Her voice broke. 'When you looked into my eyes and let me think you loved me? Was it all a lie? Every time you made love to me, did you have to force yourself to touch me in order to trick me into marrying you? Not because you wanted me for your wife, but so that you would have a legal claim to our child.'

He hesitated—and his silence spoke volumes.

'I'm right, aren't I?' Marnie's knees sagged and she almost collapsed, but pride held her upright, and when Leandro put his arms out as if he would catch her, sheer, incandescent rage swept over her.

'*Cara...*'

'*No!*'

If he touched her she knew she would succumb—because she loved him still. And that was the worst thing of all—the realisation that she was a pathetic fool like her mother had been, to love a man who did not love her.

A moan escaped from her lips—a terrible, keening sob that revealed her utter devastation.

'For God's sake, Marnie,' Leandro said roughly. He knew he would be haunted by that agonised cry for ever.

She swayed on her feet and he was afraid for her safety.

'At least let me help you down the stairs, and when you are calmer we'll talk.' Panic cramped in his gut when she shook her head wildly. 'We can work this out.'

'*Get away from me.*' Appalled by her weak longing for him to take her in his arms—*after all he had done*—she lifted the hand in which she was holding her wedding bouquet and lashed out at him.

He inhaled sharply as a thorn that had been left on a rose stem sliced across his face.

Breathing hard, Marnie stared at the line of blood that sprang up on his cheek and watched white rose petals from the broken flowers float to the floor like a ghastly mimicry of confetti.

'You once told me that I would never be your wife,' she said in a low, tightly controlled voice that was somehow more intense than if she had ranted and raved. 'You're absolutely right. I never will be. I will never forgive you, and nothing you could do or say would persuade me to marry you. I never want to see you again.'

'Maybe you don't, but we *are* going to have a child,' Leandro reminded her.

As if she needed reminding of the reason why he had been prepared to dupe her into marrying him, she thought bitterly.

'*I* am going to have a child, but *you* won't be involved.' She shot the words at him like bullets from a gun. 'I meant what I said. I never want to see you again. And if you try to find me, if you hound me and my child, I will go to court and tell a judge that you offered me money to sell you the baby, and that when I refused you took advantage of my amnesia and tried to trick me into marrying you.'

She thought of how her mother had cried for days, for weeks, after her father had left and the memory stoked her fury. She would *not* waste her life crying over Leandro, she vowed fiercely. He did not deserve her love and *she* deserved much more than to be the convenient bride of a man who did not love her.

'You're becoming hysterical. I understand why you are angry, but for the baby's sake you have to get yourself under control.'

Marnie became aware that her heart was beating painfully hard and dangerously fast. At her last antenatal appointment the nurse had said that her blood pressure was slightly raised— heaven knew how high it was now. Just as suddenly as it had swept over her the white-hot rage that had consumed her died away, and she could not hold back the tears that slid down her cheeks.

'Let me take care of you,' Leandro said softly, breaking her heart all over again.

'Leave me alone.' She could barely speak because her whole body was racked with sobs.

She didn't know what to do. Her nose was running, and when she wiped a hand over her wet eyes she saw black streaks of mascara and knew she must look like a clown. The pain in her head was making her feel sick, and panic made her breath come in shallow gasps as she faced the ultimate humiliation of throwing up at Leandro's feet.

As if from a long way off, she heard him speak.

'Marnie, I need to take you to hospital. You're in shock after regaining your memory.' He curled his fingers around her wrist and ignored her desperate cry. 'Let me help you.'

'It seems to me that you've done enough.' Uncle Brian came to stand beside Marnie and put his arm protectively around her shoulders.

He was several inches shorter than Leandro, but something about the older man's steady demeanour made Leandro look away in shame.

He watched Marnie's uncle lead her back up

the stairs. The sound of her weeping hurt him in a way he had never experienced before—as if his heart had been ripped out of his chest. His gamble had failed spectacularly, and he was beginning to realise that he had lost something so precious and priceless that he had not even considered its value until now.

She had loved him. But he had thrown her love away. And now she had demanded that he keep away from her and their child. She had said he was a monster, and she was right. What kind of man would offer the mother of his child money to give up her parental rights? *A man like his father*—the answer hit Leandro hard. With sudden insight he saw the similarities between himself and Silvestro, and he hated what he saw almost as much as he hated himself.

Marnie was innocent of every terrible thing he had accused her of. She was not a liar, nor a cheat, nor a thief. She had gifted him her virginity and had remained true to him. *Dio*, she had given him her heart. And he had stamped on it like a spoiled child in the throes of a temper tantrum—*twice*.

He watched her walk away from him and knew he deserved to lose her—but he could not accept that he would. 'I know you hate me,' he called after her. 'But this isn't just about us and our relationship. You have to think about what the baby needs.'

She had reached the top stair and she turned to look down at him. Despite the black streaks of make-up smeared across her white face she looked heartbreakingly beautiful and utterly heartbroken.

'We don't *have* a relationship. That's what you once told me,' she reminded him. 'And I *am* thinking of the baby,' Marnie continued, in a hard voice that Leandro had never heard her use before. 'For our child's sake I intend to go as far away as possible from you, because you are cruel and manipulative and those are *not* the qualities of a good father.' She tugged her engagement ring from her finger. 'You can have this back. It's beautiful to look at but completely soulless—just like you.'

She threw the ring at him and the huge diamond glittered as it sailed through the air before landing with a thud at Leandro's feet.

She turned her back on him and started to walk along the corridor. Fear curled icy fingers around Leandro's heart. She was leaving him and he could not stop her.

He was hurtled back in time to when he was seven years old, following his mother down the hall and pleading with her to stay with him. *'Don't leave me!'* he had cried when he was a boy. Now he was a man and he cried the same words silently inside himself. He wanted to run after Marnie and pull her into his arms, but he did not have any right to beg her to stay with him after the terrible way he had treated her.

For the first time he took an unblinkered view of his behaviour and he was appalled.

He spoke to Marnie's uncle. 'Look after her... please...' His voice was gruff and his throat felt as if he had swallowed broken glass. 'I assume you will take Marnie to your home in Norfolk? I'll come and see her in a few days, when we are all feeling calmer.' His jaw hardened. 'It's my baby too.'

Maybe he had lost Marnie, and maybe—definitely—he did not deserve her. But he would fight for his child and he would never give up.

'Marnie, love, you need to try and stop crying,' Aunt Susan said gently. 'You've cried for the whole journey from London to Norfolk and it can't be good for the baby that you are in such a state.'

Her aunt's words broke through the mantle of misery that had swamped Marnie since she had discovered the shattering truth of Leandro's deception. He did not love her. He had never loved her. She had been such a fool.

Yet more tears filled her eyes, but she forced herself to sit up straight in the back of the car and blew her nose on a tissue her aunt handed her.

'You'll stay with us, of course, for as long as you like.' Aunt Susan's tone became fierce. 'I hope Leandro *does* visit in a couple of days, as he said he would. I'd like to tell him exactly what I think of him.'

'I don't want to see him.' Panic surged through

Marnie. 'I never want to see Leandro again.' She did not dare. She couldn't trust herself not to be charmed by him, she acknowledged with self-disgust. Nothing could excuse Leandro's behaviour. He had lied to her repeatedly, destroyed her trust and he did not deserve a second chance.

'I can't stay with you and Uncle Brian if Leandro might turn up,' she told her aunt urgently. 'I need to go somewhere where he won't find me while I think about what I am going to do once the baby is born.'

Her aunt hesitated before she opened her handbag and took out a letter. 'Your father wrote to me a few weeks ago and asked after you. I wrote back and told him that you were expecting a baby and about to get married. Yesterday this letter arrived, addressed to you. I was going to wait until after the wedding to give it to you.'

With a trembling hand, Marnie took the envelope.

'Your dad said in his letter to me that he would love to see you again,' Aunt Susan murmured. 'Perhaps you could visit him in Bulgaria?'

CHAPTER TEN

THE WIND BLOWING off the sea whipped the tops of the sand dunes and stirred the marram grasses so that the slender fronds whispered to one another. Marnie huddled deeper into her coat, glad that her woollen hat and gloves gave her some protection from the icy January air. She liked to get out of the house and stretch her legs with a walk along the beach. Not that she was able to walk very far or fast now that she was so heavy with her child.

She felt like a lumbering hippopotamus. But there was not long to go now. The baby was due in three weeks, and she was enjoying this final part of her pregnancy. It was such a special time, and she loved staying on the remote north Norfolk coast. She had not seen another person for several days, and it felt as though it was just her and her baby bump alone in the bleakly beautiful landscape.

Her thoughts drifted to a very different landscape. The village in the mountains of Bulgaria where her father lived would be a winter wonderland, with thick snow on the ground and piled on the roofs of the houses like icing on a Christmas cake.

Visiting her father and his wife and two children—half-siblings whom she had never met before—had been strangely cathartic. Marnie hadn't known what to expect when she'd walked through the arrivals hall of the airport in Bulgaria, but despite not having seen her dad for twelve years she had recognised him instantly, and he had swept her into a bear hug. He had been just as she remembered him, funny and easy-going, and his wife and the two children—Katya and Ben—had made Marnie feel welcome.

'Things had got so bad between your mum and me that I thought the family would be better off without me,' her father had explained. 'The constant rows and your mother's accusations that I was unfaithful made a bad atmosphere for you and the twins. It's not an excuse, but your mum's obsessive jealousy drove me away.' He'd sighed. 'I tried to keep in touch with you, but it seemed like you didn't want to talk to me.'

'I felt disloyal to Mum when I spoke to you on the phone,' Marnie had admitted. 'I suppose I blamed you for making her unhappy. All she wanted was for you to love her.'

As she'd spoken the words Marnie had recognised that she was the same as her mother. Wanting Leandro to love her had been the most important thing in her life.

'Your mum mistrusted me because she lacked self-confidence and didn't believe she was worthy of being loved. But you can't make another person responsible for your happiness. You have to love yourself and believe that you deserve to be loved in order to have an equal relationship where there is respect and trust on both sides.'

Thinking of what her father had said, Marnie acknowledged that her relationship with Leandro had not been equal. She had been too amenable and too anxious to please him. She had lost respect for herself.

She watched the herring gulls swooping above the white-crested waves before she turned back to the remote wooden beach house half-hidden among the dunes that had been her home for the past week. As she drew nearer she noticed a figure standing at the top of the path leading to the cottage. Marnie occasionally saw birdwatchers on the beach, but something about the watchful stance of this figure put her on high alert.

It could not be him, she assured herself. But even from across the beach her body recognised Leandro and her heart slammed against her ribs. For a moment she was tempted to run away, but the baby kicked and reminded her that running wasn't an option in her advanced state of pregnancy. Nor did she *need* to run from Leandro. He could not hurt her any more than he had already done. She had spent the last two and a half months getting over him. She *had*.

It was a steep climb up the sloping path, and she was flushed and out of breath when she halted a few feet away from Leandro. He was wearing a sheepskin jacket with the collar pulled up around his face and he looked ruggedly sexy.

But when Marnie studied him more closely she was shocked by how thin and drawn his face was. His previously cropped hair was no longer in a sleek style and had grown down past his collar. Several days' growth of dark stubble covered his jaw. But it was his eyes that shocked her most. They were as dull as the grey winter sky and as bleak as the lonely beach. He looked as if he had spent the past months in hell and her heart softened.

Stop that, she ordered herself firmly. She would *not* let him work his magic on her again.

'I don't believe my aunt and uncle would have told you where I'm staying, so how did you find me?'

His eyes narrowed, as if he was surprised by her aggressive tone, and there was a curious huskiness in his deep voice when he replied. 'I found this house a couple of weeks after you did your disappearing act.' He exhaled heavily, and his warm breath formed a white cloud in the freezing air. 'I remembered you had once told me that your aunt and uncle owned a beach house in Norfolk. I couldn't blame them for refusing to tell me where the house was, but it was easy to check with the land registry and find the address.'

He dug his hands deeper into his pockets and did not take his eyes from her face.

'I rushed to Norfolk, hoping to talk to you, but you weren't here and the house was shut up. It still seemed like my best bet, and I haunted this place, but you never came—until now. When I arrived today and saw a car parked by the house I prayed you were here.'

'I can't imagine why you went to so much effort. I have nothing to say to you.'

'There is a lot I need to say to *you*. I want to explain—'

'But I don't want to listen.'

She cut him off abruptly, and again a flicker of surprise crossed his face. When they had been together she had always hung on his every word, Marnie remembered grimly.

'I no longer care what you want, Leandro. In the past I tried too hard to please you and make you happy. You knew I loved you and you used my feelings for you to manipulate me. But I have seen the man you really are, and I don't love you now, so I'm afraid you'll have to find some other pathetic fool to play your mind games with.'

'I never thought you were pathetic.'

She shrugged. 'I really don't care.' Tiredness swept over her, as it often did these days. She stepped round Leandro and walked towards the house. 'I assume you wanted to find me to check that the baby is okay? There are no problems with my pregnancy and the baby is fine, so you can go. I'll phone you in a few weeks, when your son or daughter has been born.'

She heard his breath hiss between his teeth and when she opened the front door he was right behind her.

He wedged his shoulder against the doorframe. 'I'm not going anywhere, *cara*. I'm staying.'

'The hell you are. I don't want you here.'

Anger and panic combined in a rush of temper. It was all very well to tell herself she was over him when she had not seen him for months, but now he was here, more gorgeous and more heartbreakingly handsome than she remembered, she had to protect herself against his dangerous charisma.

Leandro's grey eyes gleamed with steely resolve. 'When I arrived I was concerned that you didn't answer my knock on the door. I phoned your aunt and she guessed you had gone for a walk on the beach. She told me that she and your uncle are worried about you living alone, miles from the nearest town, when the baby is due soon.'

'I'm fine. Aunt Susan lives less than an hour away. When I feel the first signs that I'm in labour I'll phone her and she will come and drive me to the hospital. Everyone says that first babies take hours to arrive.'

'Are you going to risk the baby's welfare simply to score a point over me?' Leandro carefully squeezed past her into the porch. 'For your aunt and uncle's sake, if not mine, let me stay and take care of you.'

'I don't need to be taken care of.' Marnie hated the way her heart leapt at the gentleness in his voice.

She sat down on the bench and struggled to bend down over her swollen belly to unlace her boots.

'You are heavily pregnant. Of course you need someone to look after you and keep you safe,' he murmured as he knelt down in front of her and removed her boots.

She should demand that he leave, but right now she did not have the energy for a fight, Marnie acknowledged. She pulled off her hat and felt his eyes on the thick braid of hair that slipped down over her shoulder. Ignoring him, she walked into the open-plan living room. The white-painted walls and big windows made it a bright room even on a dull winter's day, and the glowing embers from the log burner added warmth and cheer.

She threw another log into the burner before taking off her coat, and grimaced when she turned round and saw the expression on Leandro's face as he stared at her.

At this late stage of her pregnancy, her leggings and a soft grey wool jumper dress were comfortable, but definitely not stylish, and she knew she looked enormous. 'This is what thirty-seven weeks pregnant looks like—get over it,' she said waspishly.

'You look beautiful.'

She ordered herself to ignore the husky note in his voice that tugged on her emotions. 'Forget the charm offensive. I'm the size of a double-decker bus, but I don't mind.' She placed her hand on the hard swell of her stomach. 'I love being pregnant and knowing that the baby will be a healthy weight when he or she is born.'

Leandro shrugged out of his sheepskin jacket and walked around the breakfast bar into the kitchen area. He filled the kettle and opened cupboard doors until he located mugs.

'Tea or coffee? Do you want something to eat? I make a mean omelette.'

'Just a cup of tea, please.' Marnie's legs ached from her walk and she sank down on the sofa in front of the fire. In a minute she would tell him he had to leave. But it was nice to be fussed over…nice not to be on her own, a traitorous voice in her heart whispered.

Her deep sigh was unconsciously wistful as

she watched Leandro. He was wearing jeans and a cream jumper that moulded his powerful chest. His over-long hair gleamed like raw silk and she longed to run her fingers through it.

He walked over, carrying a tray with their drinks and a packet of biscuits, and after he had placed the tray down on the coffee table he sat down next to her—too close for Marnie's comfort. He smelled divine… The spicy fragrance of his aftershave was evocative, and she closed her eyes to try and block out her mental image of his naked, tanned, muscular body, his limbs entwined with hers.

'My ex-wife hated being pregnant. She said it ruined her figure.'

Marnie's eyes flew open as his words registered and she jerked her head towards him.

'You were *married*?'

'Briefly. Before our second wedding anniversary Nicole and I both knew we had made a mistake,' he said drily.

'But…you have a *child*?' She was so shocked she could barely speak, and her confusion grew when Leandro shook his head. 'You said your wife was pregnant.'

'Not with *my* child, unfortunately.'

He sipped his drink and turned his eyes towards her.

'I met Nicole soon after my mother died.' He shrugged. 'Maybe I was looking for love because when I was growing up I believed that my mother cared about her career more than she loved me. Whatever the reason, I fell for Nicole hard, and when she told me she was pregnant I was keen to marry her. But cracks started to appear early in the marriage. I was busy establishing Vialli Entertainment, and although Nicole enjoyed spending the money I earned she resented the long hours I spent working for it.'

Leandro's voice hardened.

'Our divorce was reasonably amicable, and we agreed to share custody of Henry, whom I believed was my son.'

'How did you discover that Henry wasn't yours?'

'A few years after the divorce there were rumours that Nicole was having an affair with an English politician. I didn't think much of it, because my ex-wife was free to do what she liked. But Henry was growing up and there were comments—particularly from my father—that Henry looked nothing like me. I loved my son, and I couldn't believe that Nicole would have deliberately deceived me. But finally I couldn't ignore my doubts, and a DNA test revealed that I wasn't Henry's father.'

Marnie heard the raw note of pain in Leandro's voice and her soft heart ached as she imagined how he must have felt when he had received the devastating news. 'Did Nicole know that you were not her child's father?'

'Oh, yes, she always knew that her politician lover, Dominic Chilton, was Henry's real father.' Leandro did not hide his bitterness. 'But Chilton was married, and he was scared that a scandal about his mistress giving birth to his illegitimate child would ruin his political career. So, with his agreement, Nicole deceived me into thinking that Henry was my son. When I learned the truth I couldn't simply walk away from the little boy who had grown up believing I was his dad,' Leandro said gruffly. 'Once a month I used to visit Henry in Paris, where he was at school. Now Chilton has left politics and he is divorced from his wife. He and Nicole have gone public with their affair and they are taking Henry to Australia with them to start a new life.'

And in a few weeks Leandro would start a new life as father to their baby, Marnie thought. After the terrible deception by his first wife it was understandable why he had wanted proof that the child she was carrying was his. She felt the baby wriggle and watched the outline of a tiny fist or foot move beneath her jumper. From Leandro's sudden stiffness she knew his eyes were fixed on her stomach too, and instinctively she grabbed his hand and placed it on the hard mound of her belly just in time for him to feel a few hard kicks.

'Whether the baby is a boy or girl, I think it will be a future footballer,' she quipped, wanting to lighten the intense atmosphere in the room.

Leandro's hand felt heavy on her, and it seemed to burn through her clothes and set her skin on fire. It seemed a lifetime ago that she had lain in his arms and felt his hands on her naked body as he had aroused her with tender caresses and prepared her for his possession. She felt a familiar tingle in her breasts and between her legs and despaired at her weakness where this man was concerned. His revelation that his ex-wife had duped him into thinking he had a son was an explanation for his behaviour, but it did not excuse it.

The room was full of shadows. The light faded quickly in the short days of winter, and Marnie suddenly felt chilled and hauled herself to her feet to go and put another log in the stove. Through the window she watched a huge yellow moon slowly rise over the sea.

'Why didn't you tell me that your trips to Paris were to visit Henry?'

'We did not have the kind of relationship where we talked about personal matters.'

Marnie gave a pained laugh. 'What you mean is that you regarded me as your mistress and all you require from a mistress is sex. The only time you paid me any attention was in bed.'

'That's not true. In Florence—'

'Florence was different,' she snapped, whirling round to glare at him. 'Don't think I haven't worked it out, Leandro. You took me to Florence so that you could cold-bloodedly seduce me into believing that our marriage would be for real, when in fact you knew it would be a sham that you had to trick me into so that you could have legal rights to your child.'

He stood up and walked over to her, his jaw hardening when she tensed and wrapped her arms over her distended stomach, as though to protect their child from him.

'I know it looks that way—'

She interrupted him again. 'It looks that way because it *was* that way. You seized your chance when you learned of my amnesia and I bet you prayed that I would never regain my memory. But as an insurance policy you acted like a loving fiancé in Florence and hoped I would fall so deeply under your spell that even if I did remember how badly you had treated me I would forgive you.'

A dull flush flared along Leandro's sharp cheekbones. Marnie's voice had never been so cold towards him before. He knew she had every right to be angry with him, yet he hadn't really expected her to be so furious. It was a measure of his arrogance that he had assumed she would forgive him, he thought with grim self-derision.

'I admit that at the beginning everything you have said was true. I had proof that the child you were carrying was mine and I was determined to marry you. But things changed in Florence.'

'Please don't insult my intelligence by saying you fell in *love* with me in Florence.' She delivered the words in a hard voice that he was beginning to recognise as belonging to the new Marnie—the Marnie he had made her become, Leandro realised.

'We became friends in Florence, didn't we?' he said softly.

'Friends don't lie and scheme to get their own way. You omitted to tell me that I had been offered an internship with NASA because you didn't want me to take the baby to California and continue my studies—even though you knew it was my dream to have a career as an astronomer.'

Leandro knew he deserved the note of disgust he heard in her voice, but he hadn't expected it to hurt so much. It would have been better if she'd shouted at him. Anything would be better than her coldness, which was as bitter as the winter wind that whipped the Norfolk coast.

'I did what I thought was best for the baby. My mother abandoned me for her career and I didn't want our child to feel the same sense of rejection I'd felt when I was a kid.'

Her eyes flashed. 'I would *never* abandon my baby. Not for any reason. I accepted from the minute I found out I was pregnant that I would have to put my career dreams on hold while I focused on being a mother. Everything you have done you did for *you*, and what *you* wanted, so don't try to blame the baby for the fact that you behaved like a jerk. The only reason you are here now is because it's what *you* want, and if you really cared about my welfare you would go away and leave me alone.'

Marnie was breathing hard and her heart was beating too fast. Leandro's shocked expression made her want to cry. She had thought it would feel good to tell him her opinion of him, but the colour had drained from his face and the life had drained from his eyes. He did *not* look vulnerable, she told herself. He did *not* look hurt. She didn't want to picture him as a little boy, growing up without his mother. And there was an odd constriction in her throat as she imagined him having to say goodbye to the boy he had brought up as his son for six years now Henry's real father was taking him to live in Australia.

'I'm sorry,' he said after a long time. His voice was ragged, as if he had swallowed broken glass. 'I can't tell you how sorry I am for...' He closed his eyes briefly, as if they were aching with tears just as Marnie's eyes ached. 'For everything. I wish I hadn't hurt you, and because I know you don't want me here I wish I could do as you ask and go away. But I can't leave you alone in this remote place, and I assume you will refuse to allow me to take you back to London.'

When she gave a jerky nod of her head he continued.

'So I will unload my stuff from the car and

then I'll cook us both dinner—and if you don't want to speak to me I'll understand. But believe me, *cara*, you can't despise me as much as I despise myself.'

CHAPTER ELEVEN

SURPRISINGLY THAT NIGHT Marnie slept better than she had done for weeks. Probably it was due to the big dinner she had eaten, she told herself, for Leandro had proved to be an unexpectedly good cook. But deep in her heart she acknowledged that she had slept peacefully knowing that he was staying in the bedroom above her.

Her pregnant shape made her too cumbersome to climb the narrow staircase to the upper floor of the cottage, and she was unaware that Leandro now lay in the narrow single bed in the upstairs bedroom nursing a headache from where he had collided with a low ceiling beam.

He felt a far worse ache in his chest as he replayed all that Marnie had said to him over in his mind. He thought how ironic it was that he had never experienced failure in business, but now, when it came to the only thing that mattered—the one thing he had discovered that he cared about—failure to persuade Marnie to give him a second chance was a terrifying possibility.

'I didn't know you could cook,' she said two days later as they finished the delicious Thai curry Leandro had made for their evening meal.

'I don't need to in London, because my house-keeper prepares all my meals, and at the Villa Collina I have an excellent chef. But I learned to cook from the chef my father employed when I was growing up in New York. It's a useful skill to have—especially when the nearest takeaway is a good ten miles away,' he said drily, referring to the cottage's remote location.

Leandro took an appreciative sip of red wine and exhaled a slow, careful breath when Marnie smiled. Since that first explosive confrontation, when she had wiped the floor with him, the tension between them had miraculously lessened, and although she wasn't exactly chatty, she no longer spoke to him in a voice that dripped ice.

'I *love* the fact that the cottage is miles from

anywhere. It would be a lovely place for a child to grow up, with the huge beach for a back garden.'

It was the first time she had made any reference to the plans she might be thinking of for the future, and where she might want to live once the baby was born. Leandro had his own hopes for the future, but he knew he must be patient and take things slowly in his plan to win Marnie back.

'Where did you go when you left London? I despaired that I would never find you.'

'I went to Bulgaria and stayed with my father and his wife and their two children.' Marnie sensed his surprise and darted a glance at him across the table. 'It was good to spend some time with Dad. I had missed him, and he was upset that we had lost contact for so long. He would like to meet Jake too, but I don't know where he is.'

Marnie's voice faltered as she remembered that her brother had stolen the jewellery from the safe in Leandro's house and had since disappeared.

'Your brother is working as a groundsman in Scotland, as he originally planned to do,' Leandro surprised her by saying—and then he shocked her even further. 'As a matter of fact Jake and my father spent Christmas with me in London, which was not something I'd ever envisaged,' he said wryly.

'You celebrated Christmas with *Jake*...and *your father*?'

'"Celebrated" is a bit of an overstatement. I wasn't in the mood for celebrations.' He took pity on her obvious confusion. 'Your brother came to my house in Eaton Square again, because he wanted to apologise to you for stealing the jewellery—which I have already told you he had returned. Of course you weren't there, and I was drunk at two o'clock in the afternoon. I was drunk pretty much twenty-four-seven then,' Leandro admitted. 'I couldn't face that I had screwed up so badly with you, and when I told Jake what I had done I wouldn't have blamed him if he'd thumped me. Instead he realised how bad a state I was in and he found my father's phone number and called him, unaware that Silvestro was the last person I would turn to for help.'

He shook his head, as if he couldn't quite believe the chain of events that had followed.

'I was stunned when my father arrived from New York, and then between him and your brother they stopped me drowning my misery in malt Scotch and ordered me to stop feeling sorry for myself. I had more conversations with my father in a week that I'd done in thirty-odd years.'

Leandro cast his mind back to the strangest Christmas he had ever spent. He had formed a firm friendship with Jake, and he'd also learned a lot about Silvestro.

'My father never stopped loving my mother, you know,' he told Marnie. 'I'd always believed he hated her, but he admitted that he was devastated when she went on tour with her musical theatre company. He was jealous of her career. He wanted her to stay at home and just be his wife. After she left he wanted to go after her and ask her to give their marriage another try, but he was too proud to fight for her. Instead he shut himself off from emotions, from love. He has always seemed so cold, but I discovered that he has feelings—he's simply been unable to show his emotions for fear of being hurt again.'

Leandro recalled the conversation he'd had with his father.

'Pride is a damnable thing,' Silvestro had said. *'I knew I had been wrong to insist that your mother choose between her career and me when I should have been more supportive of her dreams. But my pride wouldn't let me go after her and beg her to give me another chance. Life is a lonely journey without love.'*

His father had given Leandro a searching look.

'You're proud—like me. But if something is worth fighting for then forget your pride and follow your heart.'

His heart had brought him to a windy corner of Norfolk, Leandro brooded. He was willing to fight for what he wanted, but he was by no means certain of winning the prize he wanted more than anything in life.

Simply because a truce had been established between her and Leandro it did not mean that she was falling for him again, Marnie assured herself one morning as she lay in bed and sipped the cup of tea he had brought her.

It was eight days since he had insisted on moving into the beach house to take care of her in the final weeks of her pregnancy and he had been true to his word. He had cooked meals and cleaned the cottage, refusing to allow her to lift a finger—much to her frustration, because in the last couple of days she had developed an obsession for dusting and tidying, and was itching to rearrange the furniture in the sitting room.

'It's quite common for expectant mothers to develop a nesting instinct as the due date for the birth approaches,' the midwife had explained at Marnie's antenatal appointment the previous day. 'The baby's head is engaged, which means that theoretically labour can start at any time.'

Marnie had taken this news with a sense of calm, but it had sent Leandro into panic mode.

'I wish you would come to London with me,' he said when he strode into her bedroom to ask if she wanted more tea. 'If my meeting wasn't so important I would cancel it and stay here with you.'

'I'll be fine on my own for twenty-four hours,' she assured him. 'You've said you will come back tomorrow.'

'I've changed my mind. I'm going to drive back to Norfolk as soon as the meeting finishes later today.' Leandro let out a frustrated sigh. 'I'm worried about leaving you. The midwife said you could go into labour at any moment.'

'She also said that with first pregnancies the baby's head can engage a month before the birth,' Marnie reminded him. 'My due date is still two weeks away. My back is aching a bit, and I'm too big and uncomfortable to want to sit in a car for a couple of hours' drive to London.'

'*Dio*, why didn't you tell me you have back-ache?' Leandro's handsome face tautened with concern as he stepped closer to the bed. 'It could mean that something is about to happen.'

'It means that I'm the size of a whale and I can't find a comfortable position to sleep in.'

Marnie saw his eyes move to the mountain of her belly beneath the sheet and wished she hadn't brought Leandro's attention to her very pregnant and very unsexy shape. A few times in the past week she had caught him looking at her in a way that had made her wonder if he still desired her, but then she had caught sight of her reflection in the mirror and told herself she must have imagined the glint in his eyes.

She sighed and pulled the sheet up to her chin, to hide her abundant breasts. 'Go and do whatever it is you have to do for work, and don't feel you have to rush back tonight for my sake,' she muttered, bizarrely feeling close to tears at the prospect of spending a whole day without him.

Maybe it was all the hormones zooming around her body that were responsible for her mood swings.

'I will definitely be back here this evening,' Leandro assured her.

His deep voice was as soft as velvet and it caressed Marnie's senses. Her heart turned over as she studied his sculpted features. He was wearing a business suit today, and he looked suavely sophisticated and at the same time drop-dead sexy.

It was not just his voice that was soft. His eyes were no longer steely grey but had softened to the colour of woodsmoke, and something in his intent gaze made her catch her breath as he lowered his head towards her. His lips were so close to hers that she felt his warm breath graze her skin. She longed for him to kiss her, but as she swayed towards him her common sense demanded to know why she was behaving like a pathetic fool.

Was she really going to succumb to Leandro's seduction routine again? He did not want her—he wanted his baby. Hadn't she learned *anything*?

At the last second she jerked her head to one side and heard him sigh softly as he brushed his mouth against her cheek before he straightened up and walked over to the door. 'Don't do too much today, *cara*. I promise I'll be back as soon as I can.'

Fighting a strong urge to ask him to stay with her, she shrugged. 'I've learned that your promises don't mean a lot.'

It could *not* have been hurt she glimpsed in his eyes, Marnie told herself, feeling like a bitch for deliberately trying to goad him. He had been kind and solicitous all week, and had acted as if he was walking on eggshells around her, clearly not wanting to upset the tentative truce between them. But she wanted so much more. Deep down she acknowledged that she had been pushing him, trying to make him angry so that he would stop treating her as if she was made of glass and seize her in his arms and kiss her with fiery passion like he used to do.

'I accept that my past behaviour might make you doubt my word,' he said quietly. 'I can only hope that one day I will earn your trust again. Clearly I must try harder to prove that I have changed and will never take you for granted like I once did.'

He walked out of the room without giving Marnie time to respond, and a few minutes later she heard his car engine roaring to life as he drove off. Swallowing down her tears, she lay back against the pillows, telling herself she would get up in five minutes and have a shower...

She woke feeling disorientated, and a glance at the clock revealed she had slept for a couple of hours. Leandro must be almost in London by now, she thought as she swung her legs off the bed and heaved herself to her feet.

The pain that gripped her stomach sent her thoughts scattering, and she put her hand on the bedside cabinet to steady herself when another agonising spasm ripped through her. The niggling ache in her lower back that had begun last night was now a savage pain that was becoming increasingly unbearable and it made her gasp for breath.

Her labour could *not* have started, she tried to reassure herself. It was too early. The spasms must be more of the Braxton Hicks contractions that she had experienced a few times before. Only the contractions were stronger—a *lot* stronger.

Another spasm made her cry out, and at the same time she felt a sensation of wet warmth between her legs. Instinct took over from panic and she snatched up her phone. Leandro had insisted on her putting the number of the community midwife on speed dial, and Marnie gasped with a mixture of relief and pain when her call was answered on the second ring.

'If you think your waters have broken I'll call for an ambulance and I will be with you in ten minutes,' the midwife said, in a crisp but calm voice. 'Is your partner with you? You had better phone him and warn him that the baby could be on its way.'

Speeding along the motorway, Leandro cursed when he drove straight past the junction where he'd been supposed to turn off. It was fair to say that his mind was *not* on the road, he acknowledged grimly. Nor was he sparing a thought for the business meeting in London, which was the reason he had left Marnie alone at the beach house in Norfolk.

The negotiations for Vialli Entertainment to purchase an iconic theatre on Shaftsbury Avenue were at a crucial stage, but he did not give a damn about adding another theatre to his already extensive property portfolio. Nothing was more important than Marnie—so why the hell had he left her on her own at this most crucial time, when she was mere weeks away from giving birth?

With a sudden lightning-bolt revelation Leandro realised that his concern was not so much for the baby but for Marnie. When he had at last found her at the beach house, after three months of frantically searching for her, he had promised to take care of her. So what was he doing, leaving her alone for the day? He had broken another promise to her and he could not blame her for refusing to trust him.

He turned off the motorway at the next exit and parked in the service area before phoning one of his senior executives at Vialli Entertainment and instructing him to take over the negotiations for the new theatre deal. After making the call he drove on to join the motorway heading back towards Norfolk.

An hour into the journey, his phone rang. Marnie's name flashed up on the hands-free screen. She did not waste time greeting him.

'My waters have broken.' She sounded as though she was struggling to breathe and it was clearly an effort for her to speak calmly. 'The midwife has just arrived and she says the baby is on its way. There's no time for me to get to the hospital.' Her voice shook. 'Leandro... *I'm scared.*'

Santa Madre! The panic in Marnie's voice ripped the last scales from his eyes and revealed what he had been too blind, too stubborn to see clearly until now.

'*Tesoro,*' he said thickly, 'I promise everything will be all right. I'm already on my way back to you now.'

Leandro felt a searing pain in his chest, as if he had been stabbed through his heart. He would *not* break another promise to Marnie—but how could he make everything all right, as he had promised her? She was about to give birth at a remote cottage, without pain relief and all the medical facilities of a hospital.

No wonder she was scared. *Dio—he* was scared. He hated feeling so helpless, and guilt clawed in his gut. He should not have left her alone. She was so precious. He was a bloody fool to have discovered what she meant to him so late.

Now the baby was about to be born and there was no time to convince Marnie that she was more important to him than anything—even his child.

* * *

Everything was happening so fast. *Too* fast. Through a blur of pain and confusion Marnie was struggling to concentrate on the instructions the midwife was giving her.

'I'm having another contraction,' she managed to say, before pain tore through her with the force of a tidal wave and she could not think or speak—only feel the agonising spasms that seemed as if they would rip her body apart.

'You're doing wonderfully, Marnie. It won't be long before the baby is here,' the midwife told her.

But Marnie barely heard her. Overwhelmed by the force of the contraction, she gave a desperate cry. Almost as soon as the pain faded another contraction started and she struggled to take a breath. She felt as if she was drowning.

Consumed by pain and fear she cried out again—a harsh, animal noise that surely had not come from her? Her brain recognised a noise from outside the window. A car engine. Oh, God, was Leandro here? She prayed he was. She needed him.

Tears streamed down Marnie's face as she remembered how she had snapped at Leandro as he was about to leave for London. She had wanted to hurt him as he had hurt her. But she had hurt herself, because despite everything that had happened she still loved him. It had taken until now, when her body was being torn apart by pain, for her to acknowledge that she had never stopped loving him.

Bursting through the front door of the cottage, Leandro halted in the hallway when he heard Marnie give a guttural cry that chilled his blood.

'Cara!'

He hurried into the bedroom and saw her on the bed, leaning against the pillows, her head thrown back as she let out another heart-rending cry.

'Dio!' His eyes flicked to the midwife, standing at the end of the bed. 'She is in agony. Can't you do something? Give her something to help with the pain?'

'I'm afraid it's too late for pain relief,' the midwife said calmly. 'Marnie is coping incredibly well, and you have arrived just in time to see your baby being born.'

Marnie groaned. 'I'm having another contraction. *Oh!* I can't bear it. Leandro, make it stop.'

Leandro would willingly have given everything he owned to swap places with Marnie and bear the rigours of childbirth for her.

For a few seconds he felt utterly helpless, but then he took hold of her hand and pressed his lips to her fingers. 'Squeeze my hand every time you feel a contraction. I'm here with you, *cara*, and I promise I will help you as much as I can.'

The pain did not abate, but Marnie's fear lessened now that Leandro was with her. She gripped his hand when the next contraction came and was glad of the cool flannel he held to her sweat-damp brow.

She felt an overwhelming urge to push. 'Don't you want to see your baby being born?' she gasped.

He shook his head and looked intently into her eyes. 'I promised I would stay with *you*.'

He watched her expression change, and the knife blade in his heart twisted deeper when she gave a loud moan as she began to push their child into the world.

A lifetime later—or so it seemed to Leandro—Marnie took a deep breath and, with a primal groan he knew he would never forget, delivered their baby.

'Congratulations—you have a little girl,' the midwife announced as she lifted up the infant.

Even then, Leandro's gaze remained focused on Marnie, and he watched the weariness disappear from her face to be replaced with a look of utter joy when the baby gave a shrill cry.

'A girl! Oh, Leandro, we have a daughter.'

Trembling from exhaustion and emotion, Marnie held out her arms and the midwife placed the little bundle wrapped in a white shawl to her breast. A tiny face peeped out from beneath a mass of fair hair.

'Oh…' Marnie forgot the pain of her labour as she fell instantly and irrevocably in love with her daughter. 'She's so beautiful.'

Leandro looked then, and his heart turned over. He swallowed convulsively and through a mist of tears he studied his daughter and knew that miracles truly did happen.

'Isn't she the loveliest thing you've ever seen?' Marnie whispered, entranced by the infant. 'She's perfect.'

'Yes,' Leandro agreed gruffly, but his gaze was on Marnie and his heart felt as though it would burst. 'Absolutely perfect.'

He wanted to take Marnie in his arms and kiss her, tell her how amazing she was, but he held back because he felt he did not have the right to intrude on these first moments when mother and child bonded. He felt excluded— but he only had himself to blame, he acknowledged heavily.

There had been an odd note in Leandro's voice that drew Marnie's attention, and she bit her lip as she watched him walk over to the window and stare out over the empty beach.

'Are you disappointed that we didn't have a boy?'

'Of course not.'

He swung round and smiled, but Marnie noticed that his smile did not reach his eyes.

'How could I be disappointed with our beautiful daughter? Have you thought of a name for her?'

'I'd like to call her Stella.'

Marnie told herself it was ridiculous to feel shy. Leandro had seen her at her most unglamorous, panting and groaning in the throes of childbirth, but she was conscious that the distance between them was wider than the room. She wished he would come over and kiss her. But why would he? He had his child, which was all he had wanted. He had never wanted *her*.

The baby stirred and she quickly blinked away her tears. She was a mother now, and whatever happened with her and Leandro in the future she was determined to do what was best for her daughter.

CHAPTER TWELVE

THEY TOOK STELLA to London when she was a few days old. Although Marnie loved the Norfolk cottage, its remote location and a series of wild winter storms that had lashed the coast had made her decide that it was safer for the baby to be at Leandro's house in Eaton Square.

It was good to be back. Betty, the housekeeper, fussed over the baby, and Leandro fussed over Marnie, showing her as much care and solicitousness as he had in the last weeks of her pregnancy. The strange awkwardness that had sprung up between them just after Stella's birth had disappeared, and sometimes Marnie wondered if she had imagined it.

Over the next six weeks the truce they had established in Norfolk developed into a deeper friendship—which she told herself was a *good* thing, because they could not skirt around the issue of custody arrangements for their daughter for ever.

The future could not be ignored, and nor could she ignore her feelings for Leandro, Marnie brooded on a sunny day in early March.

They had pushed Stella in her pram around Hyde Park, and seeing the bright yellow daffodils in bloom had made Marnie acknowledge that time was moving forward. Soon it would be time for her to move on with her life.

Walking back to Eaton Square, she glanced at Leandro as he strolled beside her. He was wearing black jeans and a matching shirt, topped with a tan leather jacket, and he looked relaxed and utterly gorgeous with his dark hair ruffled by the breeze.

Marnie felt a tug of desire in the pit of her stomach. A few days ago she'd had her six-week check-up following Stella's birth, and the doctor had asked what she planned to do about contraception. She had decided to go back on the birth control pill—mainly to prevent a reoccurrence of the menstrual migraines she'd used to suffer from. But the truth was that her current state of celibacy was the most reliable form of contraception, she thought wryly.

Much as she ached for Leandro to make love to her, she had to accept that he never would. The situation between them was too complicated. He hadn't mentioned marriage again and she told herself she was glad, because she could not accept a marriage of convenience. Nor did she want to be his mistress, which meant that she would have to suppress her longing for him to sweep her off to bed and make passionate love to her.

Her sigh was unknowingly wistful as she followed him into the house, and she was unaware that his brooding gaze lingered on her while she fed their daughter.

Leandro had thought that Marnie looked beautiful when she was pregnant, but he was astonished by how quickly she had regained her pre-pregnancy figure. She was wearing jeans and a soft pink cashmere jumper and she looked slim and sexy. Her long honey-blonde hair was caught up in a ponytail, with a few loose strands framing her lovely face.

The dull ache in his groin could be suppressed to some degree, with regular cold showers, but the ache in his heart was a permanent reminder of what a crass fool he had been, he thought with grim self-derision. He watched Marnie place their daughter in her crib. Everything he wanted was right here in the nursery, but Leandro had learned that he could not simply take what he wanted. The most important things in life had to be earned, and he was not at all sure that he had done enough to win Marnie's forgiveness.

He followed her out of the nursery and closed the door behind them.

'Can you come in here for a minute?' he said, holding open the door of the master bedroom. 'We need to talk.'

With those four words the sunny spring day turned cold and grey and Marnie's heart plummeted down to her toes. Leandro had sounded so serious. And what they needed to discuss—how they could both play a role in their daughter's life—was scarily serious. She realised that for the past six weeks she had been cocooned in a haze of post-pregnancy hormones, but reality was about to intrude and it threatened to destroy her happiness.

Since she had returned to the house she had not been in the bedroom she had once shared with Leandro, and her eyes were drawn to the big bed where they had spent long hours making love—a lifetime ago, it seemed. Twisting her fingers together anxiously, she watched him open a bedside drawer and take out a sheaf of papers. Marnie's mind flew back to when he had presented her with the prenuptial agreement that he'd wanted her to sign before their wedding, and she guessed that these documents he held out to her now set out custody arrangements for Stella.

'I thought you might find these interesting.'

She frowned when she saw that the papers were not legal documents, as she'd expected. 'Why would I be interested in rental properties in California?' She quickly skimmed through the pages: details of luxury apartments and photos of houses with pools in the garden, taken against a backdrop of a vivid blue sky.

'You will need somewhere to live if you decide to join the graduate programme with NASA.'

Leandro strolled across the room towards her, but although he appeared relaxed Marnie noted that his jaw was tense.

'I have spoken to the head of the internship programme in California and explained your situation, and they are willing to accept you as an intern starting in September this year. Stella will be eight months old by then, and I thought that you—'

He broke off when Marnie interrupted him.

'You thought *what*? That I would leave my baby behind in England with you so that I could follow my career dreams? No wonder you went to so much effort to ensure I was offered a place on the graduate programme. When I was pregnant you tried to get me to sell our baby to you, and now you think you can bribe me to give you custody of Stella.'

Marnie drew a shuddering breath and discovered that the pain of childbirth had been nothing compared to the agony of her heart shattering.

'How could you, Leandro?' she choked, unable to hold back the tears that slipped down her cheeks. 'I thought that we had become friends, but all the while you have been plotting to take my baby from me.'

She needed to get away from him before she broke down completely, but she had only taken one step towards the door when he caught hold of her arm and swung her round to face him.

'Friends?' he said, in an odd, flat voice. 'I believed we were friends too, but the fact that you think I would try to separate you from our child proves that I have failed to win back your trust.'

The bleakness in his eyes tugged on Marnie's soft heart.

'I can't blame you after the way I behaved, but I had hoped...' He gave a ragged sigh that seemed to come from the depths of his soul. 'I did not mean that you would live in California on your own. My idea was that the three of us would go—you, Stella and me—and while you are at lectures or studying I will look after our daughter.'

'But how can you take care of a baby while you are at work?' Marnie's confusion grew.

'How can you run Vialli Entertainment if you move to California?'

'I intend to step down from my position as chairman and appoint a new CEO to run the business in my place. Sure, I'll be kept up to date on developments within the company, but if I am a full-time father to Stella it will allow you to continue your studies and pursue your dream of a career in astronomy.'

'But Vialli Entertainment means everything to you.'

She wiped away her tears with trembling fingers. There was something about the way Leandro was looking at her—an intentness in his gaze that made her heart beat painfully hard. She imagined how devastated he must have been when he had discovered that Henry was not his son, and she thought she understood.

'I know how much you love our daughter if you are willing to step back from your career for her.'

'I will *give up* my career. I'll do *anything*—for *you*, Marnie,' he said softly.

She bit her lip, feeling more vulnerable than she had ever felt in her life. 'I don't understand...'

'I want you to have the chance to follow your dreams, and I know that you will do a brilliant job of combining astronomy with motherhood. I want you to be happy.'

Leandro drew a deep breath and prayed for the first time in his life.

'I love you, Marnie. I love you more than I knew it was possible to love someone.' He saw the doubtful look in her eyes and knew he must try harder to convince her. 'I love our daughter, of course. But *you* are everything to me, *tesoro*—my world, my joy, the love of my life.'

'Leandro...?' she whispered.

He heard the uncertainty in her voice and his heart stopped beating. What if he couldn't convince her that his feelings were true and he was offering her his heart? What if—despair gripped Leandro—what if Marnie rejected his love and rejected *him*?

'Ti amo, mio amore.'

Words were not enough to show her the depth of his feelings for her and he seized her in his arms and sought her mouth blindly, because his vision was blurred and he felt the unfamiliar burn of tears at the back of his throat.

'I love you.' He groaned against her lips. 'Please believe me.' His voice shook. 'Please forgive me. You loved me once, and if you let me I will spend the rest of my life trying to win your love again.'

She could allow her pride to be a barrier between them for ever, Marnie realised. Or she could find the courage to follow her heart and maybe all her dreams would come true.

She cupped Leandro's face in her hands and her heart clenched when she saw how bright his eyes were. The realisation that this big, strong man could cry because of *her* was humbling.

'You won my love right from the start,' she said softly. 'And I never stopped loving you— even when I told myself that I was weak and pathetic for loving a man who would never love me.'

'I *do* love you.' He groaned again. 'But for a long time I didn't want to admit that I was falling in love with you. It was only when you went away, after I had tried to trick you into marriage, that I realised what you meant to me. And when I found you and you were justifiably furious I was afraid that I had lost you for good.'

He brushed away her tears with his lips before he kissed her mouth, slow and sweet and so heartbreakingly tender that Marnie's last doubts disappeared and never returned.

'I wanted to punish you for not loving me,' she admitted. 'My mother wasted her life crying over my father and I was scared of being like her.'

'I promise I will never give you reason to cry,' Leandro assured her gently.

But he broke his promise immediately when he took a small box from his pocket and opened it to reveal an exquisite ring with a sparkling, star-shaped diamond.

'I chose this ring for you because it is unshowy and pure and as beautiful as you are. Will you make me the happiest man on this planet and marry me, Marnie, my love?'

She looked into his eyes and saw his love blazing for her. 'Yes,' she whispered, finding it hard to speak when there was a lump in her throat.

He slid the ring onto her finger and kissed away her tears. 'I would give you the moon and the stars if I could.'

'All I want is you and Stella. My family.' Her heart felt as if it would burst with happiness.

Once more words were not enough, and Leandro tightened his arms around her and kissed her with deepening passion before he undressed her with shaking hands and then undressed himself.

'I have wanted to do this for so long,' he murmured as he laid her on the bed and covered her body with his, caressing her with his hands and lips until she moaned softly and lifted her hips to invite his hard possession.

When he entered her it felt as new and wondrous as the very first time they had made love—and it *was* new, Marnie thought, because they were making love with their hearts as well as their bodies, and she knew that their love would last a lifetime.

EPILOGUE

THE SUN BLAZED in the cobalt-blue Californian sky as Marnie drove along the freeway in an open-top sports car, enjoying the feel of the breeze blowing her hair. She had picked up a light golden tan, and nine months after giving birth to Stella she was slimmer than she had been pre-pregnancy—thanks to the amount of swimming she did in the pool.

Leandro had arranged for them to rent a luxury villa in a quiet suburb that was only a few miles from the NASA research centre where she was studying astrophysics in the intern post-graduate programme. They had been in California for nearly two months and had settled into a routine where Marnie went to the research centre three days a week and left Stella with Leandro.

'Do you miss going to your office and making business deals?' she had asked him a few days ago, worried that he might become bored with being a stay-at-home father.

'Oh, sure,' Leandro had said mock seriously. 'I spend all day in the sunshine with my daughter, and with my gorgeous wife when she's not busy studying. Do you really think I miss sitting in an office?'

But although Leandro was a devoted father, his natural instinct for business had led him to buy a vineyard nearby, and he had asked Jake to manage the winery and the estate.

'I plan to let your brother be in charge and I'll enjoy drinking the wine,' he told Marnie. 'The vineyard is a good investment, and now that you have been assured of a job at the research centre at the end of the intern programme it looks like we will be staying in California indefinitely.'

Life could not get much better, Marnie acknowledged as she walked through the house and stepped outside to the pool area.

'Stella is becoming a real water baby,' she said as she watched the baby splashing happily in the shallow end of the pool, held safely in her father's hands.

'She's a wriggler.' Leandro lifted his daughter out of the water and kissed the tip of her nose before handing her to Marnie. 'Have you got her? She's as slippery as an eel.'

'But rather more beautiful than an eel.'

Marnie felt a familiar surge of maternal adoration for her golden-haired baby as she wrapped Stella in a towel. Her eyes moved to Leandro, and as she watched him rub a towel over his bronzed chest she felt a surge of a quite different kind. Desire turned her bones to liquid and the wicked gleam in his eyes as he stepped closer to her told her he had read her mind.

'I am doubly blessed to have two beautiful females in my life,' he said softly. 'And one benefit of swimming is that it tires our daughter out. Stella has fallen asleep on your shoulder.'

Marnie carefully placed the baby in her pram and adjusted the parasol. 'She should sleep for an hour or so.'

Her heart leapt as Leandro drew her into his arms. His skin had already dried in the sun, and when he closed his arms around her she pressed her face against his chest and heard the sudden acceleration of his heartbeat.

'Mmm…a whole hour to ourselves,' he murmured. 'I wonder how we could spend the time.'

'I have an idea.' She stood on tiptoe and sought his mouth with hers.

Their kiss was slow and sweet and then hot and urgent as he took control before he swept her up and laid her on a sun lounger.

'I hope your idea is the same as mine, *mia bella*,' he said thickly, his hands busy peeling her dress from her shoulders.

The sunlight caught the sapphire and diamond eternity ring that Marnie wore with her wedding and engagement rings. Leandro had given her the ring on the second anniversary of when they had become lovers, shortly before they had come to California. They had left Stella with Marnie's aunt, Susan, for a weekend and spent a romantic break in Prague.

Leandro sat back on his haunches and surveyed his wife's gorgeous naked body. The effect was predictable, and he groaned as his erection snagged on his swim shorts as he stripped and positioned himself over her. She smiled, and he felt his heart expand in his chest.

'My idea is to love you for eternity,' he told her, his love for her blazing in his eyes.

'Show me,' she invited.

And he did.

* * * * *

*If you enjoyed this story,
check out these other great reads from
Chantelle Shaw:
MASTER OF HER INNOCENCE
MISTRESS OF HIS REVENGE
A BRIDE WORTH MILLIONS
SHEIKH'S FORBIDDEN CONQUEST
TO WEAR HIS RING AGAIN
Available now!*

MILLS & BOON®
Large Print – January 2017

To Blackmail a Di Sione
Rachael Thomas

A Ring for Vincenzo's Heir
Jennie Lucas

Demetriou Demands His Child
Kate Hewitt

Trapped by Vialli's Vows
Chantelle Shaw

The Sheikh's Baby Scandal
Carol Marinelli

Defying the Billionaire's Command
Michelle Conder

The Secret Beneath the Veil
Dani Collins

Stepping into the Prince's World
Marion Lennox

Unveiling the Bridesmaid
Jessica Gilmore

The CEO's Surprise Family
Teresa Carpenter

The Billionaire from Her Past
Leah Ashton

1216 Rom LP

MILLS & BOON®
Large Print – February 2017

The Return of the Di Sione Wife
Caitlin Crews

Baby of His Revenge
Jennie Lucas

The Spaniard's Pregnant Bride
Maisey Yates

A Cinderella for the Greek
Julia James

Married for the Tycoon's Empire
Abby Green

Indebted to Moreno
Kate Walker

A Deal with Alejandro
Maya Blake

A Mistletoe Kiss with the Boss
Susan Meier

A Countess for Christmas
Christy McKellen

Her Festive Baby Bombshell
Jennifer Faye

The Unexpected Holiday Gift
Sophie Pembroke

MILLS & BOON®

Why shop at millsandboon.co.uk?

Each year, thousands of romance readers find their perfect read at millsandboon.co.uk. That's because we're passionate about bringing you the very best romantic fiction. Here are some of the advantages of shopping at www.millsandboon.co.uk:

* **Get new books first**—you'll be able to buy your favourite books one month before they hit the shops

* **Get exclusive discounts**—you'll also be able to buy our specially created monthly collections, with up to 50% off the RRP

* **Find your favourite authors**—latest news, interviews and new releases for all your favourite authors and series on our website, plus ideas for what to try next

* **Join in**—once you've bought your favourite books, don't forget to register with us to rate, review and join in the discussions

Visit **www.millsandboon.co.uk**
for all this and more today!